AMERICAN INDIAN STORIES

&

THE LANGUAGE OF STRING

AMERICAN INDIAN STORIES

ZITKALA-ŠA

&

THE LANGUAGE OF STRING

KIM SHUCK

Aunt Lute

San Fransisco

Aunt Lute Books, P.O. Box 410687, San Francisco, CA 94141

www.auntlute.com

Cover design: Helen Shewolfe Tseng

Text design: Sarah Lopez

Editorial: Shay Brawn and Emma Rosenbaum

Production Team: María Mínguez Arias, Isis Asare, Layia Bolden, Hunter Candrian-Velez, Fatima Jalloh, Joan Pinkvoss, and Golda Sargento.

Print ISBN: 978-1-951874-14-8

eBook ISBN: 978-1-939904-51-5

Library of Congress Cataloging-in-Publication Data

10 9 8 7 6 5 4 3 2 1

TABLE OF CONTENTS

INTRODUCING THE STORIES

Zitkala-Ša was born into a time of massacres, atrocities, and violations of treaties. She was born a Dakota woman with a French father in 1876, 14 years after the largest mass execution in United States history when 38 Dakota men were hanged in Minnesota. Seven years after her birth, the Religious Crimes Code banned Indigenous ceremonies and dances. We can't avoid these and other facts that would have had impact on her life and politics, not least because she was a powerful and lifelong advocate for the restoration of the rights of Native people. In no way did she fill the trope of a culturally mixed woman who belongs nowhere. She found ways to belong or create belonging wherever she was.

> *Here's where, in the past, my imposter syndrome would have kicked in. As a contemporary Native woman of my generation, I was told that we were all dead. I was told that in school, by teachers sometimes. It's interesting, this not existing. I have often felt like I'm a scribble in the margins of a book like this one, in the margins of history. Except, here, as a grown woman, in this time, being asked to write an intro to this book, I think I begin to understand what my experience might add. I'm not Dakota. Although I was coming of age just as the American Indian Religious Freedom Act was passed, making our dances and ceremonies legal again, I hadn't paid much attention to the Religious Crimes Code. Don't imagine for a moment that everyone complied with that bit of cultural abuse. I'm not a historian. Heck, I'm not even an academic in any real sense of the word. I'm a writer and a visual artist. So was Zitkala-Ša. We artists are thought to create entertainment, but it's more than that. We express and guide culture into the future.*

Like many young Native people of her time, Zitkala-Ša went to a boarding school. Unlike most, she wanted to go. She was in and out of schools for much of her life both as student and teacher. She studied violin and, for a time, taught music at Carlisle Indian Industrial School. Carlisle remains so notorious as an organ for forcing assimilation that there are still Native community members who remember older relatives speaking of it as if it were a dangerous monster that ate Native children. In a way it did, we can't know how many child hostages died from attending school there, but only around 750 graduated from nearly 11,000 enrolled students. Zitkala-Ša taught there until she had an article published that criticized the policy of forced assimilation. She was dismissed from her teaching position.

> *I've been asked by student journalists if I thought that Indigenous people were more than our damage. I do. I also think that that question was probably thought up in a classroom before hearing me speak, and asked before thinking. Yes, we are much more than our damage, but there has been damage and that can't be denied or erased. The policy of forced assimilation tells us that we can continue to exist as long as we change completely. Zitkala-Ša was willing to stand in her truth and face the consequences. She understood having responsibilities to culture, a valuable example in the current political climate.*

Published in 1921, *American Indian Stories* is a collection of Zitkala-Ša's impressions and understandings. In it, she offers up her joys, traumas, and rebellions. When she was writing, very little was published about the daily feelings of Native women. There is a whole genre of writing that seems to challenge the definition of the word autobiography. One example of this is a piece published in 1925 called *Autobiography of a Fox Woman* that appeared as part of a Bureau of Ethnology report. Unlike *American Indian Stories*, in *Autobiography of a Fox Woman* we never find out the name of the woman in question. Truman Michelson, who was the credited author, shared what he thought was important in the anonymous woman's story. It's still true that Native women are spoken of, spoken around, but rarely treated as narrator of their own stories. Zitkala-Ša offers us one window into the feelings of someone walking the bleeding edge of cultural shift. *American Indian Stories* offers the reader a palpable self, a curious, stubborn, creative, and mischievous self. She has presented stories from her life, and been willing to learn publicly. It's a precious gift from the past, complete with time-specific language. Keep an eye out for the dry humor; you will be rewarded.

> *In recent years I'm in the odd position of being asked for advice, or writing, or opinions that I have no business suggesting, scribbling, or offering. Any success I've had has mostly been practice and luck. I can't lay claim to any plan. My family is composed of many storytellers, most are better than I. In my childhood I was marinated in funny and words. My family is composed of many people who make things, most more talented than I. In my childhood I watched them problem-solve, solder, bake, and dazzle. I may or may not be talented. If I have a superpower it's a willingness to keep at things that interest me. Practice will sometimes make you better at things. With all of that practice, and what I hope is an appropriate amount of humility, I have offered my own essay to this volume. That offering, "The Language of String," was inspired by the way that Zitkala-Ša used her musical superpower to make space for herself and others in places that would otherwise not have allowed such space. There are years and miles between us, but for now that tactic still seems to work.*

K. Shuck
February 2026 mostly while it was raining

AMERICAN INDIAN STORIES

BY ZITKALA-ŠA

Dakota Sioux Indian

Lecturer; Author of "Old Indian Legends," "Americanize The First American," and other stories; Member of the Woman's National Foundation, League of American Pen-Women, and the Washington Salon

"There is no great; there is no small; in the mind that causeth all"

THIS BOOK SHOULD BE IN EVERY HOME

Old Indian Legends

25 Seminole Avenue, Forest Hill, L.I., N.Y.,
August 25, 1919.

Dear Zitkala-Sa:

I thank you for your book on Indian legends. I have read them with exquisite pleasure. Like all folk tales they mirror the child life of the world. There is in them a note of wild, strange music.

You have translated them into our language in a way that will keep them alive in the hearts of men. They are so young, so fresh, so full of the odors of the virgin forest untrod by the foot of white man! The thoughts of your people seem dipped in the colors of the rainbow, palpitant with the play of winds, eerie with the thrill of a spirit-world unseen but felt and feared.

Your tales of birds, beast, tree and spirit can not but hold captive the hearts of all children. They will kindle in their young minds that eternal wonder which creates poetry and keeps life fresh and eager. I wish you and your little book of Indian tales all success.

I am always
Sincerely your friend,
(Signed) HELEN KELLER.

CONTENTS

IMPRESSIONS OF AN INDIAN CHILDHOOD

I. My Mother

A wigwam of weather-stained canvas stood at the base of some irregularly ascending hills. A footpath wound its way gently down the sloping land till it reached the broad river bottom; creeping through the long swamp grasses that bent over it on either side, it came out on the edge of the Missouri.

Here, morning, noon, and evening, my mother came to draw water from the muddy stream for our household use. Always, when my mother started for the river, I stopped my play to run along with her. She was only of medium height. Often she was sad and silent, at which times her full arched lips were compressed into hard and bitter lines, and shadows fell under her black eyes. Then I clung to her hand and begged to know what made the tears fall.

"Hush; my little daughter must never talk about my tears"; and smiling through them, she patted my head and said, "Now let me see how fast you can run today." Whereupon I tore away at my highest possible speed, with my long black hair blowing in the breeze.

I was a wild little girl of seven. Loosely clad in a slip of brown buckskin, and light-footed with a pair of soft moccasins on my feet, I was as free as the wind that blew my hair, and no less spirited than a bounding deer. These were my mother's pride,—my wild freedom and overflowing spirits. She taught me no fear save that of intruding myself upon others.

Having gone many paces ahead I stopped, panting for breath, and laughing with glee as my mother watched my every movement. I was not wholly conscious of myself, but was more keenly alive to the fire within. It was as if I were the activity, and my hands and feet were only experiments for my spirit to work upon.

Returning from the river, I tugged beside my mother, with my hand upon the bucket I believed I was carrying. One time, on such a return, I remember a bit of conversation we had. My grown-up cousin, Warca-Ziwin (Sunflower), who was then seventeen, always went to the river alone for water for her mother. Their wigwam was not far from ours; and I saw her daily going to and from the river. I admired my cousin greatly. So I said: "Mother, when I am tall as my cousin Warca-Ziwin, you shall not have to come for water. I will do it for you."

With a strange tremor in her voice which I could not understand, she answered, "If the paleface does not take away from us the river we drink."

"Mother, who is this bad paleface?" I asked.

"My little daughter, he is a sham,—a sickly sham! The bronzed Dakota is the only real man."

I looked up into my mother's face while she spoke; and seeing her bite her lips, I knew she was unhappy. This aroused revenge in my small soul. Stamping my foot on the earth, I cried aloud, "I hate the paleface that makes my mother cry!"

Setting the pail of water on the ground, my mother stooped, and stretching her left hand out on the level with my eyes, she placed her other arm about me; she pointed to the hill where my uncle and my only sister lay buried.

"There is what the paleface has done! Since then your father too has been buried in a hill nearer the rising sun. We were once very happy. But the paleface has stolen our lands and driven us hither. Having defrauded us of our land, the paleface forced us away.

"Well, it happened on the day we moved camp that your sister and uncle were both very sick. Many others were ailing, but there seemed to be no help. We traveled many days and nights; not in the grand, happy way that we moved camp when I was a little girl, but we were driven, my child, driven like a herd of buffalo. With every step, your sister, who was not as large as you are now, shrieked with the painful jar until she was hoarse with crying. She grew more and more feverish. Her little hands and cheeks were burning hot. Her little lips were parched and dry, but she would not drink the water I gave her. Then I discovered that her throat was swollen and red. My poor child, how I cried with her because the Great Spirit had forgotten us!

"At last, when we reached this western country, on the first weary night your sister died. And soon your uncle died also, leaving a widow and an orphan daughter, your cousin Warca-Ziwin. Both your sister and uncle might have been happy with us today, had it not been for the heartless paleface."

My mother was silent the rest of the way to our wigwam. Though I saw no tears in her eyes, I knew that was because I was with her. She seldom wept before me.

II. The Legends

During the summer days my mother built her fire in the shadow of our wigwam.

In the early morning our simple breakfast was spread upon the grass west of our tepee. At the farthest point of the shade my mother sat beside her fire, toasting a savory piece of dried meat. Near her, I sat upon my feet, eating my dried meat with unleavened bread, and drinking strong black coffee.

The morning meal was our quiet hour, when we two were entirely alone. At noon, several who chanced to be passing by stopped to rest, and to share our luncheon with us, for they were sure of our hospitality.

My uncle, whose death my mother ever lamented, was one of our nation's bravest warriors. His name was on the lips of old men when talking of the proud feats of valor; and it was mentioned by younger men, too, in connection with deeds of gallantry. Old women praised him for his kindness toward them; young women held him up as an ideal to their sweethearts. Every one loved him, and my mother worshiped his memory. Thus it happened that even strangers were sure of welcome in our lodge, if they but asked a favor in my uncle's name.

Though I heard many strange experiences related by these wayfarers, I loved best the evening meal, for that was the time old legends were told. I was always glad when the sun hung low in the west, for then my mother sent me to invite the neighboring old men and women to eat supper with us. Running all the way to the wigwams, I halted shyly at the entrances. Sometimes I stood long moments without saying a word. It was not any fear that made me so dumb when out upon such a happy errand; nor was it that I wished to withhold the invitation, for it was all I could do to observe this very proper silence. But it was a sensing of the atmosphere, to assure myself that I should not hinder other plans. My mother used to say to me, as I was almost bounding away for the old people: "Wait a moment before you invite any one. If other plans are being discussed, do not interfere, but go elsewhere."

The old folks knew the meaning of my pauses; and often they coaxed my confidence by asking, "What do you seek, little granddaughter?"

"My mother says you are to come to our tepee this evening," I instantly exploded, and breathed the freer afterwards.

"Yes, yes, gladly, gladly I shall come!" each replied. Rising at once and carrying their blankets across one shoulder, they flocked leisurely from their various wigwams toward our dwelling.

My mission done, I ran back, skipping and jumping with delight. All out of breath, I told my mother almost the exact words of the answers to my invitation. Frequently she asked, "What were they doing when you entered their tepee?" This taught me to remember all I saw at a single glance. Often I told my mother my impressions without being questioned.

While in the neighboring wigwams sometimes an old Indian woman asked me, "What is your mother doing?" Unless my mother had cautioned me not to tell, I generally answered her questions without reserve.

At the arrival of our guests I sat close to my mother, and did not leave her side without first asking her consent. I ate my supper in quiet, listening patiently to the talk of the old people, wishing all the time that they would begin the stories I loved best. At last, when I could not wait any longer, I whispered in my mother's ear, "Ask them to tell an Iktomi story, mother."

Soothing my impatience, my mother said aloud, "My little daughter is anxious to hear your legends." By this time all were through eating, and the evening was fast deepening into twilight.

As each in turn began to tell a legend, I pillowed my head in my mother's lap; and lying flat upon my back, I watched the stars as they peeped down upon me, one by one. The increasing interest of the tale aroused me, and I sat up eagerly listening to every word. The old women made funny remarks, and laughed so heartily that I could not help joining them.

The distant howling of a pack of wolves or the hooting of an owl in the river bottom frightened me, and I nestled into my mother's lap. She added some dry sticks to the open fire, and the bright flames leaped up into the faces of the old folks as they sat around in a great circle.

On such an evening, I remember the glare of the fire shone on a tattooed star upon the brow of the old warrior who was telling a story. I watched him curiously as he made his unconscious gestures. The blue star upon his bronzed forehead was a puzzle to me. Looking about, I saw two parallel lines on the chin of one of the old women. The rest had none. I examined my mother's face, but found no sign there.

After the warrior's story was finished, I asked the old woman the meaning of the blue lines on her chin, looking all the while out of the corners of my eyes at the warrior with the star on his forehead. I was a little afraid that he would rebuke me for my boldness.

Here the old woman began: "Why, my grandchild, they are signs,—secret signs I dare not tell you. I shall, however, tell you a wonderful story about a woman who had a cross tattooed upon each of her cheeks."

It was a long story of a woman whose magic power lay hidden behind the marks upon her face. I fell asleep before the story was completed.

Ever after that night I felt suspicious of tattooed people. Wherever I saw one I glanced furtively at the mark and round about it, wondering what terrible magic power was covered there.

It was rarely that such a fearful story as this one was told by the camp fire. Its impression was so acute that the picture still remains vividly clear and pronounced.

III. The Beadwork.

Soon after breakfast mother sometimes began her beadwork. On a bright, clear day, she pulled out the wooden pegs that pinned the skirt of our wigwam to the ground, and rolled the canvas part way up on its frame of slender poles. Then the cool morning breezes swept freely through our dwelling, now and then wafting the perfume of sweet grasses from newly burnt prairie.

Untying the long tasseled strings that bound a small brown buckskin bag, my mother spread upon a mat beside her bunches of colored beads, just as an artist arranges the paints upon his palette. On a lapboard she smoothed out a double sheet of soft white buckskin; and drawing from a beaded case that hung on the left of her wide belt a long, narrow blade, she trimmed the buckskin into shape. Often she worked upon small moccasins for her small daughter. Then I became intensely interested in her designing. With a proud, beaming face, I watched her work. In imagination, I saw myself walking in a new pair of snugly fitting moccasins. I felt the envious eyes of my playmates upon the pretty red beads decorating my feet.

Close beside my mother I sat on a rug, with a scrap of buckskin in one hand and an awl in the other. This was the beginning of my practical observation lessons in the art of beadwork. From a skein of finely twisted threads of silvery sinews my mother pulled out a single one. With an awl she pierced the buckskin, and skillfully threaded it with the white sinew. Picking up the tiny beads one by one, she strung them with the point of her thread, always twisting it carefully after every stitch.

It took many trials before I learned how to knot my sinew thread on the point of my finger, as I saw her do. Then the next difficulty was in keeping my thread stiffly twisted, so that I could easily string my beads upon it. My mother required of me original designs for my lessons in beading. At first I frequently ensnared many a sunny hour into working a long design. Soon I learned from self-inflicted punishment to refrain from drawing complex patterns, for I had to finish whatever I began.

After some experience I usually drew easy and simple crosses and squares. These were some of the set forms. My original designs were not always symmetrical nor sufficiently characteristic, two faults with which my mother had little patience. The quietness of her oversight made me feel strongly responsible and dependent upon my own judgment. She treated me as a dignified little individual as long as I was on my good behavior; and how humiliated I was when some boldness of mine drew forth a rebuke from her!

In the choice of colors she left me to my own taste. I was pleased with an outline of yellow upon a background of dark blue, or a combination of red and myrtle-green. There was another of red with a bluish-gray that was more conventionally used. When I became a little familiar with designing and the various pleasing combinations of color, a harder lesson was given me. It was the sewing on, instead of beads, some tinted porcupine quills, moistened and flattened between the nails of the thumb and forefinger. My mother cut off the prickly ends and burned them at once in the centre fire. These sharp points were poisonous, and worked into the flesh wherever they lodged. For this reason, my mother said, I should not do much alone in quills until I was as tall as my cousin Warca-Ziwin.

Always after these confining lessons I was wild with surplus spirits, and found joyous relief in running loose in the open again. Many a summer afternoon a party of four or five of my playmates roamed over the hills with me. We each carried a light sharpened rod about four feet long, with which we pried up certain sweet roots. When we had eaten all the choice roots we chanced upon, we shouldered our rods and strayed off into patches of a stalky plant under whose yellow blossoms we found little crystal drops of gum. Drop by drop we gathered this nature's rock-candy, until each of us could boast of a lump the size of a small bird's egg. Soon satiated with its woody flavor, we tossed away our gum, to return again to the sweet roots.

I remember well how we used to exchange our necklaces, beaded belts, and sometimes even our moccasins. We pretended to offer them as gifts to one another. We delighted in impersonating our own mothers. We talked of things we had heard them say in their conversations. We imitated their various manners, even to the inflection of their voices. In the lap of the prairie we seated ourselves upon our feet, and leaning our painted cheeks in the palms of our hands, we rested our elbows on our knees, and bent forward as old women were most accustomed to do.

While one was telling of some heroic deed recently done by a near relative, the rest of us listened attentively, and exclaimed in undertones, "Han! han!" (yes! yes!) whenever the speaker paused for breath, or sometimes for our sympathy. As the discourse became more thrilling, according to our ideas, we raised our voices in these interjections. In these impersonations our parents were led to say only those things that were in common favor.

No matter how exciting a tale we might be rehearsing, the mere shifting of a cloud shadow in the landscape near by was sufficient to change our impulses; and soon we were all chasing the great shadows that played among the hills. We shouted and whooped in the chase; laughing and calling to one another, we were like little sportive nymphs on that Dakota sea of rolling green.

On one occasion I forgot the cloud shadow in a strange notion to catch up with my own shadow. Standing straight and still, I began to glide after it, putting out one foot cautiously. When, with the greatest care, I set my foot in advance of myself, my shadow crept onward too. Then again I tried it; this time with the other foot. Still again my shadow escaped me. I began to run; and away flew my shadow, always just a step beyond me. Faster and faster I ran, setting my teeth and clenching my fists, determined to overtake my own fleet shadow. But ever swifter it glided before me, while I was growing breathless and hot. Slackening my speed, I was greatly vexed that my shadow should check its pace also. Daring it to the utmost, as I thought, I sat down upon a rock imbedded in the hillside.

So! my shadow had the impudence to sit down beside me!

Now my comrades caught up with me, and began to ask why I was running away so fast.

"Oh, I was chasing my shadow! Didn't you ever do that?" I inquired, surprised that they should not understand.

They planted their moccasined feet firmly upon my shadow to stay it, and I arose. Again my shadow slipped away, and moved as often as I did. Then we gave up trying to catch my shadow.

Before this peculiar experience I have no distinct memory of having recognized any vital bond between myself and my own shadow. I never gave it an afterthought.

Returning our borrowed belts and trinkets, we rambled homeward. That evening, as on other evenings, I went to sleep over my legends.

IV. The Coffee-Making

One summer afternoon my mother left me alone in our wigwam while she went across the way to my aunt's dwelling.

I did not much like to stay alone in our tepee for I feared a tall, broad-shouldered crazy man, some forty years old, who walked loose among the hills. Wiyaka-Napbina (Wearer of a Feather Necklace) was harmless, and whenever he came into a wigwam he was driven there by extreme hunger. He went nude except for the half of a red blanket he girdled around his waist. In one tawny arm he used to carry a heavy bunch of wild sunflowers that he gathered in his aimless ramblings. His black hair was matted by the winds, and scorched into a dry red by the constant summer sun. As he took great strides, placing one brown bare foot directly in front of the other, he swung his long lean arm to and fro.

Frequently he paused in his walk and gazed far backward, shading his eyes with his hand. He was under the belief that an evil spirit was haunting his steps. This was what my mother told me once, when I sneered at such a silly big man. I was brave when my mother was near by, and Wiyaka-Napbina walking farther and farther away.

"Pity the man, my child. I knew him when he was a brave and handsome youth. He was overtaken by a malicious spirit among the hills, one day, when he went hither and thither after his ponies. Since then he can not stay away from the hills," she said.

I felt so sorry for the man in his misfortune that I prayed to the Great Spirit to restore him. But though I pitied him at a distance, I was still afraid of him when he appeared near our wigwam.

Thus, when my mother left me by myself that afternoon I sat in a fearful mood within our tepee. I recalled all I had ever heard about Wiyaka-Napbina; and I tried to assure myself that though he might pass near by, he would not come to our wigwam because there was no little girl around our grounds.

Just then, from without a hand lifted the canvas covering of the entrance; the shadow of a man fell within the wigwam, and a large roughly moccasined foot was planted inside.

For a moment I did not dare to breathe or stir, for I thought that could be no other than Wiyaka-Napbina. The next instant I sighed aloud in relief. It was an old grandfather who had often told me Iktomi legends.

"Where is your mother, my little grandchild?" were his first words.

"My mother is soon coming back from my aunt's tepee," I replied.

"Then I shall wait awhile for her return," he said, crossing his feet and seating himself upon a mat.

At once I began to play the part of a generous hostess. I turned to my mother's coffeepot.

Lifting the lid, I found nothing but coffee grounds in the bottom. I set the pot on a heap of cold ashes in the centre, and filled it half full of warm Missouri River water. During this performance I felt conscious of being watched. Then breaking off a small piece of our unleavened bread, I placed it in a bowl. Turning soon to the coffeepot, which would never have boiled on a dead fire had I waited forever, I poured out a cup of worse than muddy warm water. Carrying the bowl in one hand and cup in the other, I handed the light luncheon to the old warrior. I offered them to him with the air of bestowing generous hospitality.

"How! how!" he said, and placed the dishes on the ground in front of his crossed feet. He nibbled at the bread and sipped from the cup. I sat back against a pole watching him. I was proud to have succeeded so well in serving refreshments to a guest all by myself. Before the old warrior had finished eating, my mother entered. Immediately she wondered where I had found coffee, for she knew I had never made any, and that she had left the coffeepot empty. Answering the question in my mother's eyes, the warrior remarked, "My granddaughter made coffee on a heap of dead ashes, and served me the moment I came."

They both laughed, and mother said, "Wait a little longer, and I shall build a fire." She meant to make some real coffee. But neither she nor the warrior, whom the law of our custom had compelled to partake of my insipid hospitality, said anything to embarrass me. They treated my best judgment, poor as it was, with the utmost respect. It was not till long years afterward that I learned how ridiculous a thing I had done.

V. The Dead Man's Plum Bush.

One autumn afternoon many people came streaming toward the dwelling of our near neighbor. With painted faces, and wearing broad white bosoms of elk's teeth, they hurried down the narrow footpath to Haraka Wambdi's wigwam. Young mothers held their children by the hand, and half pulled them along in their haste. They overtook and passed by the bent old grandmothers who were trudging along with crooked canes toward the centre of excitement. Most of the young braves galloped hither on their ponies. Toothless warriors, like the old women, came more slowly, though mounted on lively ponies. They sat proudly erect on their horses. They wore their eagle plumes, and waved their various trophies of former wars.

In front of the wigwam a great fire was built, and several large black kettles of venison were suspended over it. The crowd were seated about it on the grass in a great circle. Behind them some of the braves stood leaning against the necks of their ponies, their tall figures draped in loose robes which were well drawn over their eyes.

Young girls, with their faces glowing like bright red autumn leaves, their glossy braids falling over each ear, sat coquettishly beside their chaperons. It was a custom for young Indian women to invite some older relative to escort them to the public feasts. Though it was not an iron law, it was generally observed.

Haraka Wambdi was a strong young brave, who had just returned from his first battle, a warrior. His near relatives, to celebrate his new rank, were spreading a feast to which the whole of the Indian village was invited.

Holding my pretty striped blanket in readiness to throw over my shoulders, I grew more and more restless as I watched the gay throng assembling. My mother was busily broiling a wild duck that my aunt had that morning brought over.

"Mother, mother, why do you stop to cook a small meal when we are invited to a feast?" I asked, with a snarl in my voice.

"My child, learn to wait. On our way to the celebration we are going to stop at Chanyu's wigwam. His aged mother-in-law is lying very ill, and I think she would like a taste of this small game."

Having once seen the suffering on the thin, pinched features of this dying woman, I felt a momentary shame that I had not remembered her before.

On our way I ran ahead of my mother and was reaching out my hand to pick some purple plums that grew on a small bush, when I was checked by a low "Sh!" from my mother.

"Why, mother, I want to taste the plums!" I exclaimed, as I dropped my hand to my side in disappointment.

"Never pluck a single plum from this brush, my child, for its roots are wrapped around an Indian's skeleton. A brave is buried here. While he lived he was so fond of playing the game of striped plum seeds that, at his death, his set of plum seeds were buried in his hands. From them sprang up this little bush."

Eyeing the forbidden fruit, I trod lightly on the sacred ground, and dared to speak only in whispers until we had gone many paces from it. After that time I halted in my ramblings whenever I came in sight of the plum bush. I grew sober with awe, and was alert to hear a long-drawn-out whistle rise from the roots of it. Though I had never heard with my own ears this strange whistle of departed spirits, yet I had listened so frequently to hear the old folks describe it that I knew I should recognize it at once.

The lasting impression of that day, as I recall it now, is what my mother told me about the dead man's plum bush.

VI. The Ground Squirrel

In the busy autumn days my cousin Warca-Ziwin's mother came to our wigwam to help my mother preserve foods for our winter use. I was very fond of my aunt, because she was not so quiet as my mother. Though she was older, she was more jovial and less reserved. She was slender and remarkably erect. While my mother's hair was heavy and black, my aunt had unusually thin locks.

Ever since I knew her she wore a string of large blue beads around her neck,—beads that were precious because my uncle had given them to her when she was a younger woman. She had a peculiar swing in her gait, caused by a long stride rarely natural to so slight a figure. It was during my aunt's visit with us that my mother forgot her accustomed quietness, often laughing heartily at some of my aunt's witty remarks.

I loved my aunt threefold: for her hearty laughter, for the cheerfulness she caused my mother, and most of all for the times she dried my tears and held me in her lap, when my mother had reproved me.

Early in the cool mornings, just as the yellow rim of the sun rose above the hills, we were up and eating our breakfast. We awoke so early that we saw the sacred hour when a misty smoke hung over a pit surrounded by an impassable sinking mire. This strange smoke appeared every morning, both winter and summer; but most visibly in midwinter it rose immediately above the marshy spot. By the time the full face of the sun appeared above the eastern horizon, the smoke vanished. Even very old men, who had known this country the longest, said that the smoke from this pit had never failed a single day to rise heavenward.

As I frolicked about our dwelling I used to stop suddenly, and with a fearful awe watch the smoking of the unknown fires. While the vapor was visible I was afraid to go very far from our wigwam unless I went with my mother.

From a field in the fertile river bottom my mother and aunt gathered an abundant supply of corn. Near our tepee they spread a large canvas upon the grass, and dried their sweet corn in it. I was left to watch the corn, that nothing should disturb it. I played around it with dolls made of ears of corn. I braided their soft fine silk for hair, and gave them blankets as various as the scraps I found in my mother's workbag.

There was a little stranger with a black-and-yellow-striped coat that used to come to the drying corn. It was a little ground squirrel, who was so fearless of me that he came to one corner of the canvas and carried away as much of the sweet corn as he could hold.

I wanted very much to catch him and rub his pretty fur back, but my mother said he would be so frightened if I caught him that he would bite my fingers. So I was as content as he to keep the corn between us. Every morning he came for more corn. Some evenings I have seen him creeping about our grounds; and when I gave a sudden whoop of recognition he ran quickly out of sight.

When mother had dried all the corn she wished, then she sliced great pumpkins into thin rings; and these she doubled and linked together into long chains. She hung them on a pole that stretched between two forked posts. The wind and sun soon thoroughly dried the chains of pumpkin. Then she packed them away in a case of thick and stiff buckskin.

In the sun and wind she also dried many wild fruits,—cherries, berries, and plums. But chiefest among my early recollections of autumn is that one of the corn drying and the ground squirrel.

I have few memories of winter days at this period of my life, though many of the summer. There is one only which I can recall.

Some missionaries gave me a little bag of marbles. They were all sizes and colors. Among them were some of colored glass. Walking with my mother to the river, on a late winter day, we found great chunks of ice piled all along the bank. The ice on the river was floating in huge pieces. As I stood beside one large block, I noticed for the first time the colors of the rainbow in the crystal ice. Immediately I thought of my glass marbles at home. With my bare fingers I tried to pick out some of the colors, for they seemed so near the surface. But my fingers began to sting with the intense cold, and I had to bite them hard to keep from crying.

From that day on, for many a moon, I believed that glass marbles had river ice inside of them.

VII. The Big Red Apples

The first turning away from the easy, natural flow of my life occurred in an early spring. It was in my eighth year; in the month of March, I afterward learned. At this age I knew but one language, and that was my mother's native tongue.

From some of my playmates I heard that two paleface missionaries were in our village. They were from that class of white men who wore big hats and carried large hearts, they said. Running direct to my mother, I began to question her why these two strangers were among us. She told me, after I had teased much, that they had come to take away Indian boys and girls to the East. My mother did not seem to want me to talk about them. But in a day or two, I gleaned many wonderful stories from my playfellows concerning the strangers.

"Mother, my friend Judéwin is going home with the missionaries. She is going to a more beautiful country than ours; the palefaces told her so!" I said wistfully, wishing in my heart that I too might go.

Mother sat in a chair, and I was hanging on her knee. Within the last two seasons my big brother Dawée had returned from a three years' education in the East, and his coming back influenced my mother to take a farther step from her native way of living. First it was a change from the buffalo skin to the white man's canvas that covered our wigwam. Now she had given up her wigwam of slender poles, to live, a foreigner, in a home of clumsy logs.

"Yes, my child, several others besides Judéwin are going away with the palefaces. Your brother said the missionaries had inquired about his little sister," she said, watching my face very closely.

My heart thumped so hard against my breast, I wondered if she could hear it.

"Did he tell them to take me, mother?" I asked, fearing lest Dawée had forbidden the palefaces to see me, and that my hope of going to the Wonderland would be entirely blighted.

With a sad, slow smile, she answered: "There! I knew you were wishing to go, because Judéwin has filled your ears with the white man's lies. Don't believe a word they say! Their words are sweet, but, my child, their deeds are bitter. You will cry for me, but they will not even soothe you. Stay with me, my little one! Your brother Dawée says that going East, away from your mother, is too hard an experience for his baby sister."

Thus my mother discouraged my curiosity about the lands beyond our eastern horizon; for it was not yet an ambition for Letters that was stirring me. But on the following day the missionaries did come to our very house. I spied them coming up the footpath leading to our cottage. A third man was with them, but he was not my brother Dawée. It was another, a young interpreter, a paleface who had a smattering of the Indian language. I was ready to run out to meet them, but I did not dare to displease my mother. With great glee, I jumped up and down on our ground floor. I begged my mother to open the door, that they would be sure to come to us. Alas! They came, they saw, and they conquered!

Judéwin had told me of the great tree where grew red, red apples; and how we could reach out our hands and pick all the red apples we could eat. I had never seen apple trees. I had never tasted more than a dozen red apples in my life; and when I heard of the orchards of the East, I was eager to roam among them. The missionaries smiled into my eyes and patted my head. I wondered how mother could say such hard words against him.

"Mother, ask them if little girls may have all the red apples they want, when they go East," I whispered aloud, in my excitement.

The interpreter heard me, and answered: "Yes, little girl, the nice red apples are for those who pick them; and you will have a ride on the iron horse if you go with these good people."

I had never seen a train, and he knew it.

"Mother, I am going East! I like big red apples, and I want to ride on the iron horse! Mother, say yes!" I pleaded.

My mother said nothing. The missionaries waited in silence; and my eyes began to blur with tears, though I struggled to choke them back. The corners of my mouth twitched, and my mother saw me.

"I am not ready to give you any word," she said to them. "Tomorrow I shall send you my answer by my son."

With this they left us. Alone with my mother, I yielded to my tears, and cried aloud, shaking my head so as not to hear what she was saying to me. This was the first time I had ever been so unwilling to give up my own desire that I refused to hearken to my mother's voice.

There was a solemn silence in our home that night. Before I went to bed I begged the Great Spirit to make my mother willing I should go with the missionaries.

The next morning came, and my mother called me to her side. "My daughter, do you still persist in wishing to leave your mother?" she asked.

"Oh, mother, it is not that I wish to leave you, but I want to see the wonderful Eastern land," I answered.

My dear old aunt came to our house that morning, and I heard her say, "Let her try it."

I hoped that, as usual, my aunt was pleading on my side. My brother Dawée came for mother's decision. I dropped my play, and crept close to my aunt.

"Yes, Dawée, my daughter, though she does not understand what it all means, is anxious to go. She will need an education when she is grown, for then there will be fewer real Dakotas, and many more palefaces. This tearing her away, so young, from her mother is necessary, if I would have her an educated woman. The palefaces, who owe us a large debt for stolen lands, have begun to pay a tardy justice in offering some education to our children. But I know my daughter must suffer keenly in this experiment. For her sake, I dread to tell you my reply to the missionaries. Go, tell them that they may take my little daughter, and that the Great Spirit shall not fail to reward them according to their hearts."

Wrapped in my heavy blanket, I walked with my mother to the carriage that was soon to take us to the iron horse. I was happy. I met my playmates, who were also wearing their best thick blankets. We showed one another our new beaded moccasins, and the width of the belts that girdled our new dresses. Soon we were being drawn rapidly away by the white man's horses. When I saw the lonely figure of my mother vanish in the distance, a sense of regret settled heavily upon me. I felt suddenly weak, as if I might fall limp to the ground. I was in the hands of strangers whom my mother did not fully trust. I no longer felt free to be myself, or to voice my own feelings. The tears trickled down my cheeks, and I buried my face in the folds of my blanket. Now the first step, parting me from my mother, was taken, and all my belated tears availed nothing.

Having driven thirty miles to the ferryboat, we crossed the Missouri in the evening. Then riding again a few miles eastward, we stopped before a massive brick building. I looked at it in amazement, and with a vague misgiving, for in our village I had never seen so large a house. Trembling with fear and distrust of the palefaces, my teeth chattering from the chilly ride, I crept noiselessly in my soft moccasins along the narrow hall, keeping very close to the bare wall. I was as frightened and bewildered as the captured young of a wild creature.

THE SCHOOL DAYS OF AN INDIAN GIRL

I. The Land of Red Apples

There were eight in our party of bronzed children who were going East with the missionaries. Among us were three young braves, two tall girls, and we three little ones, Judéwin, Thowin, and I.

We had been very impatient to start on our journey to the Red Apple Country, which, we were told, lay a little beyond the great circular horizon of the Western prairie. Under a sky of rosy apples we dreamt of roaming as freely and happily as we had chased the cloud shadows on the Dakota plains. We had anticipated much pleasure from a ride on the iron horse, but the throngs of staring palefaces disturbed and troubled us.

On the train, fair women, with tottering babies on each arm, stopped their haste and scrutinized the children of absent mothers. Large men, with heavy bundles in their hands, halted near by, and riveted their glassy blue eyes upon us.

I sank deep into the corner of my seat, for I resented being watched. Directly in front of me, children who were no larger than I hung themselves upon the backs of their seats, with their bold white faces toward me. Sometimes they took their forefingers out of their mouths and pointed at my moccasined feet. Their mothers, instead of reproving such rude curiosity, looked closely at me, and attracted their children's further notice to my blanket. This embarrassed me, and kept me constantly on the verge of tears.

I sat perfectly still, with my eyes downcast, daring only now and then to shoot long glances around me. Chancing to turn to the window at my side, I was quite breathless upon seeing one familiar object. It was the telegraph pole which strode by at short paces. Very near my mother's dwelling, along the edge of a road thickly bordered with wild sunflowers, some poles like these had been planted by white men. Often I had stopped, on my way down the road, to hold my ear against the pole, and, hearing its low moaning, I used to wonder what the paleface had done to hurt it. Now I sat watching for each pole that glided by to be the last one.

In this way I had forgotten my uncomfortable surroundings, when I heard one of my comrades call out my name. I saw the missionary standing very near, tossing candies and gums into our midst. This amused us all, and we tried to see who could catch the most of the sweetmeats. The missionary's generous distribution of candies was impressed upon my memory by a disastrous result which followed. I had caught more than my share of candies and gums, and soon after our arrival at the school I had a chance to disgrace myself, which, I am ashamed to say, I did.

Though we rode several days inside of the iron horse, I do not recall a single thing about our luncheons.

It was night when we reached the school grounds. The lights from the windows of the large buildings fell upon some of the icicled trees that stood beneath them. We were led toward an open door, where the brightness of the lights within flooded out over the heads of the excited palefaces who blocked our way. My body trembled more from fear than from the snow I trod upon.

Entering the house, I stood close against the wall. The strong glaring light in the large whitewashed room dazzled my eyes. The noisy hurrying of hard shoes upon a bare wooden floor increased the whirring in my ears. My only safety seemed to be in keeping next to the wall. As I was wondering in which direction to escape from all this confusion, two warm hands grasped me firmly, and in the same moment I was tossed high in midair. A rosy-cheeked paleface woman caught me in her arms. I was both frightened and insulted by such trifling. I stared into her eyes, wishing her to let me stand on my own feet, but she jumped me up and down with increasing enthusiasm. My mother had never made a plaything of her wee daughter. Remembering this I began to cry aloud.

They misunderstood the cause of my tears, and placed me at a white table loaded with food. There our party were united again. As I did not hush my crying, one of the older ones whispered to me, "Wait until you are alone in the night."

It was very little I could swallow besides my sobs, that evening.

"Oh, I want my mother and my brother Dawée! I want to go to my aunt!" I pleaded; but the ears of the palefaces could not hear me.

From the table we were taken along an upward incline of wooden boxes, which I learned afterward to call a stairway. At the top was a quiet hall, dimly lighted. Many narrow beds were in one straight line down the entire length of the wall. In them lay sleeping brown faces, which peeped just out of the coverings. I was tucked into bed with one of the tall girls, because she talked to me in my mother tongue and seemed to soothe me.

I had arrived in the wonderful land of rosy skies, but I was not happy, as I had thought I should be. My long travel and the bewildering sights had exhausted me. I fell asleep, heaving deep, tired sobs. My tears were left to dry themselves in streaks, because neither my aunt nor my mother was near to wipe them away.

II. The Cutting of My Long Hair

The first day in the land of apples was a bitter-cold one; for the snow still covered the ground, and the trees were bare. A large bell rang for breakfast, its loud metallic voice crashing through the belfry overhead and into our sensitive ears. The annoying clatter of shoes on bare floors gave us no peace. The constant clash of harsh noises, with an undercurrent of many voices murmuring an unknown tongue, made a bedlam within which I was securely tied. And though my spirit tore itself in struggling for its lost freedom, all was useless.

A paleface woman, with white hair, came up after us. We were placed in a line of girls who were marching into the dining room. These were Indian girls, in stiff shoes and closely clinging dresses. The small girls wore sleeved aprons and shingled hair. As I walked noiselessly in my soft moccasins, I felt like sinking to the floor, for my blanket had been stripped from my shoulders. I looked hard at the Indian girls, who seemed not to care that they were even more immodestly dressed than I, in their tightly fitting clothes. While we marched in, the boys entered at an opposite door. I watched for the three young braves who came in our party. I spied them in the rear ranks, looking as uncomfortable as I felt. A small bell was tapped, and each of the pupils drew a chair from under the table. Supposing this act meant they were to be seated, I pulled out mine and at once slipped into it from one side. But when I turned my head, I saw that I was the only one seated, and all the rest at our table remained standing. Just as I began to rise, looking shyly around to see how chairs were to be used, a second bell was sounded. All were seated at last, and I had to crawl back into my chair again. I heard a man's voice at one end of the hall, and I looked around to see him. But all the others hung their heads over their plates. As I glanced at the long chain of tables, I caught the eyes of a paleface woman upon me. Immediately I dropped my eyes, wondering why I was so keenly watched by the strange woman. The man ceased his mutterings, and then a third bell was tapped. Every one picked up his knife and fork and began eating. I began crying instead, for by this time I was afraid to venture anything more.

But this eating by formula was not the hardest trial in that first day. Late in the morning, my friend Judéwin gave me a terrible warning. Judéwin knew a few words of English; and she had overheard the paleface woman talk about cutting our long, heavy hair. Our mothers had taught us that only unskilled warriors who were captured had their hair shingled by the enemy. Among our people, short hair was worn by mourners, and shingled hair by cowards!

We discussed our fate some moments, and when Judéwin said, "We have to submit, because they are strong," I rebelled.

"No, I will not submit! I will struggle first!" I answered.

I watched my chance, and when no one noticed, I disappeared. I crept up the stairs as quietly as I could in my squeaking shoes,—my moccasins had been exchanged for shoes. Along the hall I passed, without knowing whither I was going. Turning aside to an open door, I found a large room with three white beds in it. The windows were covered with dark green curtains, which made the room very dim. Thankful that no one was there, I directed my steps toward the corner farthest from the door. On my hands and knees I crawled under the bed, and cuddled myself in the dark corner.

From my hiding place I peered out, shuddering with fear whenever I heard footsteps near by. Though in the hall loud voices were calling my name, and I knew that even Judéwin was searching for me, I did not open my mouth to answer. Then the steps were quickened and the voices became excited. The sounds came nearer and nearer. Women and girls entered the room. I held my breath and watched them open closet doors and peep behind large trunks. Some one threw up the curtains, and the room was filled with sudden light. What caused them to stoop and look under the bed I do not know. I remember being dragged out, though I resisted by kicking and scratching wildly. In spite of myself, I was carried downstairs and tied fast in a chair.

I cried aloud, shaking my head all the while until I felt the cold blades of the scissors against my neck, and heard them gnaw off one of my thick braids. Then I lost my spirit. Since the day I was taken from my mother I had suffered extreme indignities. People had stared at me. I had been tossed about in the air like a wooden puppet. And now my long hair was shingled like a coward's! In my anguish I moaned for my mother, but no one came to comfort me. Not a soul reasoned quietly with me, as my own mother used to do; for now I was only one of many little animals driven by a herder.

III. The Snow Episode

A short time after our arrival we three Dakotas were playing in the snowdrift. We were all still deaf to the English language, excepting Judéwin, who always heard such puzzling things. One morning we learned through her ears that we were forbidden to fall lengthwise in the snow, as we had been doing, to see our own impressions. However, before many hours we had forgotten the order, and were having great sport in the snow, when a shrill voice called us. Looking up, we saw an imperative hand beckoning us into the house. We shook the snow off ourselves, and started toward the woman as slowly as we dared.

Judéwin said: "Now the paleface is angry with us. She is going to punish us for falling into the snow. If she looks straight into your eyes and talks loudly, you must wait until she stops. Then, after a tiny pause, say, 'No.'" The rest of the way we practiced upon the little word "no."

As it happened, Thowin was summoned to judgment first. The door shut behind her with a click.

Judéwin and I stood silently listening at the keyhole. The paleface woman talked in very severe tones. Her words fell from her lips like crackling embers, and her inflection ran up like the small end of a switch. I understood her voice better than the things she was saying. I was certain we had made her very impatient with us. Judéwin heard enough of the words to realize all too late that she had taught us the wrong reply.

"Oh, poor Thowin!" she gasped, as she put both hands over her ears.

Just then I heard Thowin's tremulous answer, "No."

With an angry exclamation, the woman gave her a hard spanking. Then she stopped to say something. Judéwin said it was this: "Are you going to obey my word the next time?"

Thowin answered again with the only word at her command, "No."

This time the woman meant her blows to smart, for the poor frightened girl shrieked at the top of her voice. In the midst of the whipping the blows ceased abruptly, and the woman asked another question: "Are you going to fall in the snow again?"

Thowin gave her bad passwood another trial. We heard her say feebly, "No! No!"

With this the woman hid away her half-worn slipper, and led the child out, stroking her black shorn head. Perhaps it occurred to her that brute force is not the solution for such a problem. She did nothing to Judéwin nor to me. She only returned to us our unhappy comrade, and left us alone in the room.

During the first two or three seasons misunderstandings as ridiculous as this one of the snow episode frequently took place, bringing unjustifiable frights and punishments into our little lives.

Within a year I was able to express myself somewhat in broken English. As soon as I comprehended a part of what was said and done, a mischievous spirit of revenge possessed me. One day I was called in from my play for some misconduct. I had disregarded a rule which seemed to me very needlessly binding. I was sent into the kitchen to mash the turnips for dinner. It was noon, and steaming dishes were hastily carried into the dining-room. I hated turnips, and their odor which came from the brown jar was offensive to me. With fire in my heart, I took the wooden tool that the paleface woman held out to me. I stood upon a step, and, grasping the handle with both hands, I bent in hot rage over the turnips. I worked my vengeance upon them. All were so busily occupied that no one noticed me. I saw that the turnips were in a pulp, and that further beating could not improve them; but the order was, "Mash these turnips," and mash them I would! I renewed my energy; and as I sent the masher into the bottom of the jar, I felt a satisfying sensation that the weight of my body had gone into it.

Just here a paleface woman came up to my table. As she looked into the jar, she shoved my hands roughly aside. I stood fearless and angry. She placed her red hands upon the rim of the jar. Then she gave one lift and stride away from the table. But lo! the pulpy contents fell through the crumbled bottom to the floor! She spared me no scolding phrases that I had earned. I did not heed them. I felt triumphant in my revenge, though deep within me I was a wee bit sorry to have broken the jar.

As I sat eating my dinner, and saw that no turnips were served, I whooped in my heart for having once asserted the rebellion within me.

IV. The Devil

Among the legends the old warriors used to tell me were many stories of evil spirits. But I was taught to fear them no more than those who stalked about in material guise. I never knew there was an insolent chieftain among the bad spirits, who dared to array his forces against the Great Spirit, until I heard this white man's legend from a paleface woman.

Out of a large book she showed me a picture of the white man's devil. I looked in horror upon the strong claws that grew out of his fur-covered fingers. His feet were like his hands. Trailing at his heels was a scaly tail tipped with a serpent's open jaws. His face was a patchwork: he had bearded cheeks, like some I had seen palefaces wear; his nose was an eagle's bill, and his sharp-pointed ears were pricked up like those of a sly fox. Above them a pair of cow's horns curved upward. I trembled with awe, and my heart throbbed in my throat, as I looked at the king of evil spirits. Then I heard the paleface woman say that this terrible creature roamed loose in the world, and that little girls who disobeyed school regulations were to be tortured by him.

That night I dreamt about this evil divinity. Once again I seemed to be in my mother's cottage. An Indian woman had come to visit my mother. On opposite sides of the kitchen stove, which stood in the center of the small house, my mother and her guest were seated in straight-backed chairs. I played with a train of empty spools hitched together on a string. It was night, and the wick burned feebly. Suddenly I heard some one turn our door-knob from without.

My mother and the woman hushed their talk, and both looked toward the door. It opened gradually. I waited behind the stove. The hinges squeaked as the door was slowly, very slowly pushed inward.

Then in rushed the devil! He was tall! He looked exactly like the picture I had seen of him in the white man's papers. He did not speak to my mother, because he did not know the Indian language, but his glittering yellow eyes were fastened upon me. He took long strides around the stove, passing behind the woman's chair. I threw down my spools, and ran to my mother. He did not fear her, but followed closely after me. Then I ran round and round the stove, crying aloud for help. But my mother and the woman seemed not to know my danger. They sat still, looking quietly upon the devil's chase after me. At last I grew dizzy. My head revolved as on a hidden pivot. My knees became numb, and doubled under my weight like a pair of knife blades without a spring. Beside my mother's chair I fell in a heap. Just as the devil stooped over me with outstretched claws my mother awoke from her quiet indifference, and lifted me on her lap. Whereupon the devil vanished, and I was awake.

On the following morning I took my revenge upon the devil. Stealing into the room where a wall of shelves was filled with books, I drew forth The Stories of the Bible. With a broken slate pencil I carried in my apron pocket, I began by scratching out his wicked eyes. A few moments later, when I was ready to leave the room, there was a ragged hole in the page where the picture of the devil had once been.

V. Iron Routine

A loud-clamoring bell awakened us at half-past six in the cold winter mornings. From happy dreams of Western rolling lands and unlassoed freedom we tumbled out upon chilly bare floors back again into a paleface day. We had short time to jump into our shoes and clothes, and wet our eyes with icy water, before a small hand bell was vigorously rung for roll call.

There were too many drowsy children and too numerous orders for the day to waste a moment in any apology to nature for giving her children such a shock in the early morning. We rushed downstairs, bounding over two high steps at a time, to land in the assembly room.

A paleface woman, with a yellow-covered roll book open on her arm and a gnawed pencil in her hand, appeared at the door. Her small, tired face was coldly lighted with a pair of large gray eyes.

She stood still in a halo of authority, while over the rim of her spectacles her eyes pried nervously about the room. Having glanced at her long list of names and called out the first one, she tossed up her chin and peered through the crystals of her spectacles to make sure of the answer "Here."

Relentlessly her pencil black-marked our daily records if we were not present to respond to our names, and no chum of ours had done it successfully for us. No matter if a dull headache or the painful cough of slow consumption had delayed the absentee, there was only time enough to mark the tardiness. It was next to impossible to leave the iron routine after the civilizing machine had once begun its day's buzzing; and as it was inbred in me to suffer in silence rather than to appeal to the ears of one whose open eyes could not see my pain, I have many times trudged in the day's harness heavy-footed, like a dumb sick brute.

Once I lost a dear classmate. I remember well how she used to mope along at my side, until one morning she could not raise her head from her pillow. At her deathbed I stood weeping, as the paleface woman sat near her moistening the dry lips. Among the folds of the bedclothes I saw the open pages of the white man's Bible. The dying Indian girl talked disconnectedly of Jesus the Christ and the paleface who was cooling her swollen hands and feet.

I grew bitter, and censured the woman for cruel neglect of our physical ills. I despised the pencils that moved automatically, and the one teaspoon which dealt out, from a large bottle, healing to a row of variously ailing Indian children. I blamed the hard-working, well-meaning, ignorant woman who was inculcating in our hearts her superstitious ideas. Though I was sullen in all my little troubles, as soon as I felt better I was ready again to smile upon the cruel woman. Within a week I was again actively testing the chains which tightly bound my individuality like a mummy for burial.

The melancholy of those black days has left so long a shadow that it darkens the path of years that have since gone by. These sad memories rise above those of smoothly grinding school days. Perhaps my Indian nature is the moaning wind which stirs them now for their present record. But, however tempestuous this is within me, it comes out as the low voice of a curiously colored seashell, which is only for those ears that are bent with compassion to hear it.

VI. Four Strange Summers

After my first three years of school, I roamed again in the Western country through four strange summers.

During this time I seemed to hang in the heart of chaos, beyond the touch or voice of human aid. My brother, being almost ten years my senior, did not quite understand my feelings. My mother had never gone inside of a schoolhouse, and so she was not capable of comforting her daughter who could read and write. Even nature seemed to have no place for me. I was neither a wee girl nor a tall one; neither a wild Indian nor a tame one. This deplorable situation was the effect of my brief course in the East, and the unsatisfactory "teenth" in a girl's years.

It was under these trying conditions that, one bright afternoon, as I sat restless and unhappy in my mother's cabin, I caught the sound of the spirited step of my brother's pony on the road which passed by our dwelling. Soon I heard the wheels of a light buckboard, and Dawée's familiar "Ho!" to his pony. He alighted upon the bare ground in front of our house. Tying his pony to one of the projecting corner logs of the low-roofed cottage, he stepped upon the wooden doorstep.

I met him there with a hurried greeting, and, as I passed by, he looked a quiet "What?" into my eyes.

When he began talking with my mother, I slipped the rope from the pony's bridle. Seizing the reins and bracing my feet against the dashboard, I wheeled around in an instant. The pony was ever ready to try his speed. Looking backward, I saw Dawée waving his hand to me. I turned with the curve in the road and disappeared. I followed the winding road which crawled upward between the bases of little hillocks. Deep water-worn ditches ran parallel on either side. A strong wind blew against my cheeks and fluttered my sleeves. The pony reached the top of the highest hill, and began an even race on the level lands. There was nothing moving within that great circular horizon of the Dakota prairies save the tall grasses, over which the wind blew and rolled off in long, shadowy waves.

Within this vast wigwam of blue and green I rode reckless and insignificant. It satisfied my small consciousness to see the white foam fly from the pony's mouth.

Suddenly, out of the earth a coyote came forth at a swinging trot that was taking the cunning thief toward the hills and the village beyond. Upon the moment's impulse, I gave him a long chase and a wholesome fright. As I turned away to go back to the village, the wolf sank down upon his haunches for rest, for it was a hot summer day; and as I drove slowly homeward, I saw his sharp nose still pointed at me, until I vanished below the margin of the hilltops.

In a little while I came in sight of my mother's house. Dawée stood in the yard, laughing at an old warrior who was pointing his forefinger, and again waving his whole hand, toward the hills. With his blanket drawn over one shoulder, he talked and motioned excitedly. Dawée turned the old man by the shoulder and pointed me out to him.

"Oh, han!" (Oh, yes) the warrior muttered, and went his way. He had climbed the top of his favorite barren hill to survey the surrounding prairies, when he spied my chase after the coyote. His keen eyes recognized the pony and driver. At once uneasy for my safety, he had come running to my mother's cabin to give her warning. I did not appreciate his kindly interest, for there was an unrest gnawing at my heart.

As soon as he went away, I asked Dawée about something else.

"No, my baby sister, I cannot take you with me to the party tonight," he replied. Though I was not far from fifteen, and I felt that before long I should enjoy all the privileges of my tall cousin, Dawée persisted in calling me his baby sister.

That moonlight night, I cried in my mother's presence when I heard the jolly young people pass by our cottage. They were no more young braves in blankets and eagle plumes, nor Indian maids with prettily painted cheeks. They had gone three years to school in the East, and had become civilized. The young men wore the white man's coat and trousers, with bright neckties. The girls wore tight muslin dresses, with ribbons at neck and waist. At these gatherings they talked English. I could speak English almost as well as my brother, but I was not properly dressed to be taken along. I had no hat, no ribbons, and no close-fitting gown. Since my return from school I had thrown away my shoes, and wore again the soft moccasins.

While Dawée was busily preparing to go I controlled my tears. But when I heard him bounding away on his pony, I buried my face in my arms and cried hot tears.

My mother was troubled by my unhappiness. Coming to my side, she offered me the only printed matter we had in our home. It was an Indian Bible, given her some years ago by a missionary. She tried to console me. "Here, my child, are the white man's papers. Read a little from them," she said most piously.

I took it from her hand, for her sake; but my enraged spirit felt more like burning the book, which afforded me no help, and was a perfect delusion to my mother. I did not read it, but laid it unopened on the floor, where I sat on my feet. The dim yellow light of the braided muslin burning in a small vessel of oil flickered and sizzled in the awful silent storm which followed my rejection of the Bible.

Now my wrath against the fates consumed my tears before they reached my eyes. I sat stony, with a bowed head. My mother threw a shawl over her head and shoulders, and stepped out into the night.

After an uncertain solitude, I was suddenly aroused by a loud cry piercing the night. It was my mother's voice wailing among the barren hills which held the bones of buried warriors. She called aloud for her brothers' spirits to support her in her helpless misery.

My fingers grey icy cold, as I realized that my unrestrained tears had betrayed my suffering to her, and she was grieving for me.

Before she returned, though I knew she was on her way, for she had ceased her weeping, I extinguished the light, and leaned my head on the window sill.

Many schemes of running away from my surroundings hovered about in my mind. A few more moons of such a turmoil drove me away to the eastern school. I rode on the white man's iron steed, thinking it would bring me back to my mother in a few winters, when I should be grown tall, and there would be congenial friends awaiting me.

VII. Incurring My Mother's Displeasure

In the second journey to the East I had not come without some precautions. I had a secret interview with one of our best medicine men, and when I left his wigwam I carried securely in my sleeve a tiny bunch of magic roots. This possession assured me of friends wherever I should go. So absolutely did I believe in its charms that I wore it through all the school routine for more than a year. Then, before I lost my faith in the dead roots, I lost the little buckskin bag containing all my good luck.

At the close of this second term of three years I was the proud owner of my first diploma. The following autumn I ventured upon a college career against my mother's will.

I had written for her approval, but in her reply I found no encouragement. She called my notice to her neighbors' children, who had completed their education in three years. They had returned to their homes, and were then talking English with the frontier settlers. Her few words hinted that I had better give up my slow attempt to learn the white man's ways, and be content to roam over the prairies and find my living upon wild roots. I silenced her by deliberate disobedience.

Thus, homeless and heavy-hearted, I began anew my life among strangers.

As I hid myself in my little room in the college dormitory, away from the scornful and yet curious eyes of the students, I pined for sympathy. Often I wept in secret, wishing I had gone West, to be nourished by my mother's love, instead of remaining among a cold race whose hearts were frozen hard with prejudice.

During the fall and winter seasons I scarcely had a real friend, though by that time several of my classmates were courteous to me at a safe distance.

My mother had not yet forgiven my rudeness to her, and I had no moment for letter-writing. By daylight and lamplight, I spun with reeds and thistles, until my hands were tired from their weaving, the magic design which promised me the white man's respect.

At length, in the spring term, I entered an oratorical contest among the various classes. As the day of competition approached, it did not seem possible that the event was so near at hand, but it came. In the chapel the classes assembled together, with their invited guests. The high platform was carpeted, and gayly festooned with college colors. A bright white light illumined the room, and outlined clearly the great polished beams that arched the domed ceiling. The assembled crowds filled the air with pulsating murmurs. When the hour for speaking arrived all were hushed. But on the wall the old clock which pointed out the trying moment ticked calmly on.

One after another I saw and heard the orators. Still, I could not realize that they longed for the favorable decision of the judges as much as I did. Each contestant received a loud burst of applause, and some were cheered heartily. Too soon my turn came, and I paused a moment behind the curtains for a deep breath. After my concluding words, I heard the same applause that the others had called out.

Upon my retreating steps, I was astounded to receive from my fellow-students a large bouquet of roses tied with flowing ribbons. With the lovely flowers I fled from the stage. This friendly token was a rebuke to me for the hard feelings I had borne them.

Later, the decision of the judges awarded me the first place. Then there was a mad uproar in the hall, where my classmates sang and shouted my name at the top of their lungs; and the disappointed students howled and brayed in fearfully dissonant tin trumpets. In this excitement, happy students rushed forward to offer their congratulations. And I could not conceal a smile when they wished to escort me in a procession to the students' parlor, where all were going to calm themselves. Thanking them for the kind spirit which prompted them to make such a proposition, I walked alone with the night to my own little room.

A few weeks afterward, I appeared as the college representative in another contest. This time the competition was among orators from different colleges in our State. It was held at the State capital, in one of the largest opera houses.

Here again was a strong prejudice against my people. In the evening, as the great audience filled the house, the student bodies began warring among themselves. Fortunately, I was spared witnessing any of the noisy wrangling before the contest began. The slurs against the Indian that stained the lips of our opponents were already burning like a dry fever within my breast.

But after the orations were delivered a deeper burn awaited me. There, before that vast ocean of eyes, some college rowdies threw out a large white flag, with a drawing of a most forlorn Indian girl on it. Under this they had printed in bold black letters words that ridiculed the college which was represented by a "squaw." Such worse than barbarian rudeness embittered me. While we waited for the verdict of the judges, I gleamed fiercely upon the throngs of palefaces. My teeth were hard set, as I saw the white flag still floating insolently in the air.

Then anxiously we watched the man carry toward the stage the envelope containing the final decision.

There were two prizes given, that night, and one of them was mine!

The evil spirit laughed within me when the white flag dropped out of sight, and the hands which hurled it hung limp in defeat.

Leaving the crowd as quickly as possible, I was soon in my room. The rest of the night I sat in an armchair and gazed into the crackling fire. I laughed no more in triumph when thus alone. The little taste of victory did not satisfy a hunger in my heart. In my mind I saw my mother far away on the Western plains, and she was holding a charge against me.

AN INDIAN TEACHER AMONG INDIANS

I. My First Day

Though an illness left me unable to continue my college course, my pride kept me from returning to my mother. Had she known of my worn condition, she would have said the white man's papers were not worth the freedom and health I had lost by them. Such a rebuke from my mother would have been unbearable, and as I felt then it would be far too true to be comfortable.

Since the winter when I had my first dreams about red apples I had been traveling slowly toward the morning horizon. There had been no doubt about the direction in which I wished to go to spend my energies in a work for the Indian race. Thus I had written my mother briefly, saying my plan for the year was to teach in an Eastern Indian school. Sending this message to her in the West, I started at once eastward.

Thus I found myself, tired and hot, in a black veiling of car smoke, as I stood wearily on a street corner of an old-fashioned town, waiting for a car. In a few moments more I should be on the school grounds, where a new work was ready for my inexperienced hands.

Upon entering the school campus, I was surprised at the thickly clustered buildings which made it a quaint little village, much more interesting than the town itself. The large trees among the houses gave the place a cool, refreshing shade, and the grass a deeper green. Within this large court of grass and trees stood a low green pump. The queer boxlike case had a revolving handle on its side, which clanked and creaked constantly.

I made myself known, and was shown to my room,—a small, carpeted room, with ghastly walls and ceiling. The two windows, both on the same side, were curtained with heavy muslin yellowed with age. A clean white bed was in one corner of the room, and opposite it was a square pine table covered with a black woolen blanket.

Without removing my hat from my head, I seated myself in one of the two stiff-backed chairs that were placed beside the table. For several heart throbs I sat still looking from ceiling to floor, from wall to wall, trying hard to imagine years of contentment there. Even while I was wondering if my exhausted strength would sustain me through this undertaking, I heard a heavy tread stop at my door. Opening it, I met the imposing figure of a stately gray-haired man. With a light straw hat in one hand, and the right hand extended for greeting, he smiled kindly upon me. For some reason I was awed by his wondrous height and his strong square shoulders, which I felt were a finger's length above my head.

I was always slight, and my serious illness in the early spring had made me look rather frail and languid. His quick eye measured my height and breadth. Then he looked into my face. I imagined that a visible shadow flitted across his countenance as he let my hand fall. I knew he was no other than my employer.

"Ah ha! so you are the little Indian girl who created the excitement among the college orators!" he said, more to himself than to me. I thought I heard a subtle note of disappointment in his voice. Looking in from where he stood, with one sweeping glance, he asked if I lacked anything for my room.

After he turned to go, I listened to his step until it grew faint and was lost in the distance. I was aware that my car-smoked appearance had not concealed the lines of pain on my face.

For a short moment my spirit laughed at my ill fortune, and I entertained the idea of exerting myself to make an improvement. But as I tossed my hat off a leaden weakness came over me, and I felt as if years of weariness lay like water-soaked logs upon me. I threw myself upon the bed, and, closing my eyes, forgot my good intention.

II. A Trip Westward

One sultry month I sat at a desk heaped up with work. Now, as I recall it, I wonder how I could have dared to disregard nature's warning with such recklessness. Fortunately, my inheritance of a marvelous endurance enabled me to bend without breaking.

Though I had gone to and fro, from my room to the office, in an unhappy silence, I was watched by those around me. On an early morning I was summoned to the superintendent's office. For a half-hour I listened to his words, and when I returned to my room I remembered one sentence above the rest. It was this: "I am going to turn you loose to pasture!" He was sending me West to gather Indian pupils for the school, and this was his way of expressing it.

I needed nourishment, but the midsummer's travel across the continent to search the hot prairies for overconfident parents who would entrust their children to strangers was a lean pasturage. However, I dwelt on the hope of seeing my mother. I tried to reason that a change was a rest. Within a couple of days I started toward my mother's home.

The intense heat and the sticky car smoke that followed my homeward trail did not noticeably restore my vitality. Hour after hour I gazed upon the country which was receding rapidly from me. I noticed the gradual expansion of the horizon as we emerged out of the forests into the plains. The great high buildings, whose towers overlooked the dense woodlands, and whose gigantic clusters formed large cities, diminished, together with the groves, until only little log cabins lay snugly in the bosom of the vast prairie. The cloud shadows which drifted about on the waving yellow of long-dried grasses thrilled me like the meeting of old friends.

At a small station, consisting of a single frame house with a rickety board walk around it, I alighted from the iron horse, just thirty miles from my mother and my brother Dawée. A strong hot wind seemed determined to blow my hat off, and return me to olden days when I roamed bareheaded over the hills. After the puffing engine of my train was gone, I stood on the platform in deep solitude. In the distance I saw the gently rolling land leap up into bare hills. At their bases a broad gray road was winding itself round about them until it came by the station. Among these hills I rode in a light conveyance, with a trusty driver, whose unkempt flaxen hair hung shaggy about his ears and his leather neck of reddish tan. From accident or decay he had lost one of his long front teeth.

Though I call him a paleface, his cheeks were of a brick red. His moist blue eyes, blurred and bloodshot, twitched involuntarily. For a long time he had driven through grass and snow from this solitary station to the Indian village. His weather-stained clothes fitted badly his warped shoulders. He was stooped, and his protruding chin, with its tuft of dry flax, nodded as monotonously as did the head of his faithful beast.

All the morning I looked about me, recognizing old familiar sky lines of rugged bluffs and round-topped hills. By the roadside I caught glimpses of various plants whose sweet roots were delicacies among my people. When I saw the first cone-shaped wigwam, I could not help uttering an exclamation which caused my driver a sudden jump out of his drowsy nodding.

At noon, as we drove through the eastern edge of the reservation, I grew very impatient and restless. Constantly I wondered what my mother would say upon seeing her little daughter grown tall. I had not written her the day of my arrival, thinking I would surprise her. Crossing a ravine thicketed with low shrubs and plum bushes, we approached a large yellow acre of wild sunflowers. Just beyond this nature's garden we drew near to my mother's cottage. Close by the log cabin stood a little canvas-covered wigwam. The driver stopped in front of the open door, and in a long moment my mother appeared at the threshold.

I had expected her to run out to greet me, but she stood still, all the while staring at the weather-beaten man at my side. At length, when her loftiness became unbearable, I called to her, "Mother, why do you stop?"

This seemed to break the evil moment, and she hastened out to hold my head against her cheek.

"My daughter, what madness possessed you to bring home such a fellow?" she asked, pointing at the driver, who was fumbling in his pockets for change while he held the bill I gave him between his jagged teeth.

"Bring him! Why, no, mother, he has brought me! He is a driver!" I exclaimed.

Upon this revelation, my mother threw her arms about me and apologized for her mistaken inference. We laughed away the momentary hurt. Then she built a brisk fire on the ground in the tepee, and hung a blackened coffeepot on one of the prongs of a forked pole which leaned over the flames. Placing a pan on a heap of red embers, she baked some unleavened bread. This light luncheon she brought into the cabin, and arranged on a table covered with a checkered oilcloth.

My mother had never gone to school, and though she meant always to give up her own customs for such of the white man's ways as pleased her, she made only compromises. Her two windows, directly opposite each other, she curtained with a pink-flowered print. The naked logs were unstained, and rudely carved with the axe so as to fit into one another. The sod roof was trying to boast of tiny sunflowers, the seeds of which had probably been planted by the constant wind. As I leaned my head against the logs, I discovered the peculiar odor that I could not forget. The rains had soaked the earth and roof so that the smell of damp clay was but the natural breath of such a dwelling.

"Mother, why is not your house cemented? Do you have no interest in a more comfortable shelter?" I asked, when the apparent inconveniences of her home seemed to suggest indifference on her part.

"You forget, my child, that I am now old, and I do not work with beads any more. Your brother Dawée, too, has lost his position, and we are left without means to buy even a morsel of food," she replied.

Dawée was a government clerk in our reservation when I last heard from him. I was surprised upon hearing what my mother said concerning his lack of employment. Seeing the puzzled expression on my face, she continued: "Dawée! Oh, has he not told you that the Great Father at Washington sent a white son to take your brother's pen from him? Since then Dawée has not been able to make use of the education the Eastern school has given him."

I found no words with which to answer satisfactorily. I found no reason with which to cool my inflamed feelings.

Dawée was a whole day's journey off on the prairie, and my mother did not expect him until the next day. We were silent.

When, at length, I raised my head to hear more clearly the moaning of the wind in the corner logs, I noticed the daylight streaming into the dingy room through several places where the logs fitted unevenly. Turning to my mother, I urged her to tell me more about Dawée's trouble, but she only said: "Well, my daughter, this village has been these many winters a refuge for white robbers. The Indian cannot complain to the Great Father in Washington without suffering outrage for it here. Dawée tried to secure justice for our tribe in a small matter, and today you see the folly of it."

Again, though she stopped to hear what I might say, I was silent.

"My child, there is only one source of justice, and I have been praying steadfastly to the Great Spirit to avenge our wrongs," she said, seeing I did not move my lips.

My shattered energy was unable to hold longer any faith, and I cried out desperately: "Mother, don't pray again! The Great Spirit does not care if we live or die! Let us not look for good or justice: then we shall not be disappointed!"

"Sh! my child, do not talk so madly. There is Taku Iyotan Wasaka,[1] 12to which I pray," she answered, as she stroked my head again as she used to do when I was a smaller child.

III. My Mother's Curse Upon White Settlers

One black night mother and I sat alone in the dim starlight, in front of our wigwam. We were facing the river, as we talked about the shrinking limits of the village. She told me about the poverty-stricken white settlers, who lived in caves dug in the long ravines of the high hills across the river.

A whole tribe of broad-footed white beggars had rushed hither to make claims on those wild lands. Even as she was telling this I spied a small glimmering light in the bluffs.

"That is a white man's lodge where you see the burning fire," she said. Then, a short distance from it, only a little lower than the first, was another light. As I became accustomed to the night, I saw more and more twinkling lights, here and there, scattered all along the wide black margin of the river.

Still looking toward the distant firelight, my mother continued: "My daughter, beware of the paleface. It was the cruel paleface who caused the death of your sister and your uncle, my brave brother. It is this same paleface who offers in one palm the holy papers, and with the other gives a holy baptism of firewater. He is the hypocrite

---

1. An absolute Power.

who reads with one eye, 'Thou shalt not kill,' and with the other gloats upon the sufferings of the Indian race." Then suddenly discovering a new fire in the bluffs, she exclaimed, "Well, well, my daughter, there is the light of another white rascal!"

She sprang to her feet, and, standing firm beside her wigwam, she sent a curse upon those who sat around the hated white man's light. Raising her right arm forcibly into line with her eye, she threw her whole might into her doubled fist as she shot it vehemently at the strangers. Long she held her outstretched fingers toward the settler's lodge, as if an invisible power passed from them to the evil at which she aimed.

IV. Retrospection

Leaving my mother, I returned to the school in the East. As months passed over me, I slowly comprehended that the large army of white teachers in Indian schools had a larger missionary creed than I had suspected.

It was one which included self-preservation quite as much as Indian education. When I saw an opium-eater holding a position as teacher of Indians, I did not understand what good was expected, until a Christian in power replied that this pumpkin-colored creature had a feeble mother to support. An inebriate paleface sat stupid in a doctor's chair, while Indian patients carried their ailments to untimely graves, because his fair wife was dependent upon him for her daily food.

I find it hard to count that white man a teacher who tortured an ambitious Indian youth by frequently reminding the brave changeling that he was nothing but a "government pauper."

Though I burned with indignation upon discovering on every side instances no less shameful than those I have mentioned, there was no present help. Even the few rare ones who have worked nobly for my race were powerless to choose workmen like themselves. To be sure, a man was sent from the Great Father to inspect Indian schools, but what he saw was usually the students' sample work *made* for exhibition. I was nettled by this sly cunning of the workmen who hoodwinked the Indian's pale Father at Washington.

My illness, which prevented the conclusion of my college course, together with my mother's stories of the encroaching frontier settlers, left me in no mood to strain my eyes in searching for latent good in my white co-workers.

At this stage of my own evolution, I was ready to curse men of small capacity for being the dwarfs their God had made them. In the process of my education I had lost all consciousness of the nature world about me. Thus, when a hidden rage took me to the small white-walled prison which I then called my room, I unknowingly turned away from my one salvation.

Alone in my room, I sat like the petrified Indian woman of whom my mother used to tell me. I wished my heart's burdens would turn me to unfeeling stone. But alive, in my tomb, I was destitute!

For the white man's papers I had given up my faith in the Great Spirit. For these same papers I had forgotten the healing in trees and brooks. On account of my mother's simple view of life, and my lack of any, I gave her up, also. I made no friends among the race of people I loathed. Like a slender tree, I had been uprooted from my mother, nature, and God. I was shorn of my branches, which had waved in sympathy and love for home and friends. The natural coat of bark which had protected my oversensitive nature was scraped off to the very quick.

Now a cold bare pole I seemed to be, planted in a strange earth. Still, I seemed to hope a day would come when my mute aching head, reared upward to the sky, would flash a zigzag lightning across the heavens. With this dream of vent for a long-pent consciousness, I walked again amid the crowds.

At last, one weary day in the schoolroom, a new idea presented itself to me. It was a new way of solving the problem of my inner self. I liked it. Thus I resigned my position as teacher; and now I am in an Eastern city, following the long course of study I have set for myself. Now, as I look back upon the recent past, I see it from a distance, as a whole. I remember how, from morning till evening, many specimens of civilized peoples visited the Indian school. The city folks with canes and eyeglasses, the countrymen with sunburnt cheeks and clumsy feet, forgot their relative social ranks in an ignorant curiosity. Both sorts of these Christian palefaces were alike astounded at seeing the children of savage warriors so docile and industrious.

As answers to their shallow inquiries they received the students' sample work to look upon. Examining the neatly figured pages, and gazing upon the Indian girls and boys bending over their books, the white visitors walked out of the schoolhouse well satisfied: they were educating the children of the red man! They were paying a liberal fee to the government employees in whose able hands lay the small forest of Indian timber.

In this fashion many have passed idly through the Indian schools during the last decade, afterward to boast of their charity to the North American Indian. But few there are who have paused to question whether real life or long-lasting death lies beneath this semblance of civilization.

WHY I AM A PAGAN

When the spirit swells my breast I love to roam leisurely among the green hills; or sometimes, sitting on the brink of the murmuring Missouri, I marvel at the great blue overhead. With half-closed eyes I watch the huge cloud shadows in their noiseless play upon the high bluffs opposite me, while into my ear ripple the sweet, soft cadences of the river's song. Folded hands lie in my lap, for the time forgot. My heart and I lie small upon the earth like a grain of throbbing sand. Drifting clouds and tinkling waters, together with the warmth of a genial summer day, bespeak with eloquence the loving Mystery round about us. During the idle while I sat upon the sunny river brink, I grew somewhat, though my response be not so clearly manifest as in the green grass fringing the edge of the high bluff back of me.

At length retracing the uncertain footpath scaling the precipitous embankment, I seek the level lands where grow the wild prairie flowers. And they, the lovely little folk, soothe my soul with their perfumed breath.

Their quaint round faces of varied hue convince the heart which leaps with glad surprise that they, too, are living symbols of omnipotent thought. With a child's eager eye I drink in the myriad star shapes wrought in luxuriant color upon the green. Beautiful is the spiritual essence they embody.

I leave them nodding in the breeze, but take along with me their impress upon my heart. I pause to rest me upon a rock embedded on the side of a foothill facing the low river bottom. Here the Stone-Boy, of whom the American aborigine tells, frolics about, shooting his baby arrows and shouting aloud with glee at the tiny shafts of lightning that flash from the flying arrow-beaks. What an ideal warrior he became, baffling the siege of the pests of all the land till he triumphed over their united attack. And here he lay—Inyan our great-great-grandfather, older than the hill he rested on, older than the race of men who love to tell of his wonderful career.

Interwoven with the thread of this Indian legend of the rock, I fain would trace a subtle knowledge of the native folk which enabled them to recognize a kinship to any and all parts of this vast universe. By the leading of an ancient trail I move toward the Indian village.

With the strong, happy sense that both great and small are so surely enfolded in His magnitude that, without a miss, each has his allotted individual ground of opportunities, I am buoyant with good nature.

Yellow Breast, swaying upon the slender stem of a wild sunflower, warbles a sweet assurance of this as I pass near by. Breaking off the clear crystal song, he turns his wee head from side to side eyeing me wisely as slowly I plod with moccasined feet. Then again he yields himself to his song of joy. Flit, flit hither and yon, he fills the summer sky with his swift, sweet melody. And truly does it seem his vigorous freedom lies more in his little spirit than in his wing.

With these thoughts I reach the log cabin whither I am strongly drawn by the tie of a child to an aged mother. Out bounds my four-footed friend to meet me, frisking about my path with unmistakable delight. Chän is a black shaggy dog, "a thoroughbred little mongrel" of whom I am very fond. Chän seems to understand many words in Sioux, and will go to her mat even when I whisper the word, though generally I think she is guided by the tone of the voice. Often she tries to imitate the sliding inflection and long-drawn-out voice to the amusement of our guests, but her articulation is quite beyond my ear. In both my hands I hold her shaggy head and gaze into her large brown eyes. At once the dilated pupils contract into tiny black dots, as if the roguish spirit within would evade my questioning.

Finally resuming the chair at my desk I feel in keen sympathy with my fellow-creatures, for I seem to see clearly again that all are akin. The racial lines, which once were bitterly real, now serve nothing more than marking out a living mosaic of human beings. And even here men of the same color are like the ivory keys of one instrument where each resembles all the rest, yet varies from them in pitch and quality of voice. And those creatures who are for a time mere echoes of another's note are not unlike the fable of the thin sick man whose distorted shadow, dressed like a real creature, came to the old master to make him follow as a shadow. Thus with a compassion for all echoes in human guise, I greet the solemn-faced "native preacher" whom I find awaiting me. I listen with respect for God's creature, though he mouth most strangely the jangling phrases of a bigoted creed.

As our tribe is one large family, where every person is related to all the others, he addressed me:—

"Cousin, I came from the morning church service to talk with you."

"Yes?" I said interrogatively, as he paused for some word from me.

Shifting uneasily about in the straight-backed chair he sat upon, he began: "Every holy day (Sunday) I look about our little God's house, and not seeing you there, I am disappointed. This is why I come today. Cousin, as I watch you from afar, I see no unbecoming behavior and hear only good reports of you, which all the more burns me with the wish that you were a church member. Cousin, I was taught long years ago by kind missionaries to read the holy book. These godly men taught me also the folly of our old beliefs.

"There is one God who gives reward or punishment to the race of dead men. In the upper region the Christian dead are gathered in unceasing song and prayer. In the deep pit below, the sinful ones dance in torturing flames.

"Think upon these things, my cousin, and choose now to avoid the after-doom of hell fire!" Then followed a long silence in which he clasped tighter and unclasped again his interlocked fingers.

Like instantaneous lightning flashes came pictures of my own mother's making, for she, too, is now a follower of the new superstition.

"Knocking out the chinking of our log cabin, some evil hand thrust in a burning taper of braided dry grass, but failed of his intent, for the fire died out and the half-burned brand fell inward to the floor. Directly above it, on a shelf, lay the holy book. This is what we found after our return from a several days' visit. Surely some great power is hid in the sacred book!"

Brushing away from my eyes many like pictures, I offered midday meal to the converted Indian sitting wordless and with downcast face. No sooner had he risen from the table with "Cousin, I have relished it," than the church bell rang.

Thither he hurried forth with his afternoon sermon. I watched him as he hastened along, his eyes bent fast upon the dusty road till he disappeared at the end of a quarter of a mile.

The little incident recalled to mind the copy of a missionary paper brought to my notice a few days ago, in which a "Christian" pugilist commented upon a recent article of mine, grossly perverting the spirit of my pen. Still I would not forget that the pale-faced missionary and the hoodooed aborigine are both God's creatures, though small indeed their own conceptions of Infinite Love. A wee child toddling in a wonder world, I prefer to their dogma my excursions into the natural gardens where the voice of the Great Spirit is heard in the twittering of birds, the rippling of mighty waters, and the sweet breathing of flowers. If this is Paganism, then at present, at least, I am a Pagan.

THE SOFT-HEARTED SIOUX

I.

Beside the open fire I sat within our tepee. With my red blanket wrapped tightly about my crossed legs, I was thinking of the coming season, my sixteenth winter. On either side of the wigwam were my parents. My father was whistling a tune between his teeth while polishing with his bare hand a red stone pipe he had recently carved. Almost in front of me, beyond the center fire, my old grandmother sat near the entranceway.

She turned her face toward her right and addressed most of her words to my mother. Now and then she spoke to me, but never did she allow her eyes to rest upon her daughter's husband, my father. It was only upon rare occasions that my grandmother said anything to him. Thus his ears were open and ready to catch the smallest wish she might express. Sometimes when my grandmother had been saying things which pleased him, my father used to comment upon them. At other times, when he could not approve of what was spoken, he used to work or smoke silently.

On this night my old grandmother began her talk about me. Filling the bowl of her red stone pipe with dry willow bark, she looked across at me.

"My grandchild, you are tall and are no longer a little boy." Narrowing her old eyes, she asked, "My grandchild, when are you going to bring here a handsome young woman?" I stared into the fire rather than meet her gaze. Waiting for my answer, she stooped forward and through the long stem drew a flame into the red stone pipe.

I smiled while my eyes were still fixed upon the bright fire, but I said nothing in reply. Turning to my mother, she offered her the pipe. I glanced at my grandmother. The loose buckskin sleeve fell off at her elbow and showed a wrist covered with silver bracelets.

Holding up the fingers of her left hand, she named off the desirable young women of our village.

"Which one, my grandchild, which one?" she questioned.

"Hoh!" I said, pulling at my blanket in confusion. "Not yet!" Here my mother passed the pipe over the fire to my father. Then she, too, began speaking of what I should do.

"My son, be always active. Do not dislike a long hunt. Learn to provide much buffalo meat and many buckskins before you bring home a wife." Presently my father gave the pipe to my grandmother, and he took his turn in the exhortations.

"Ho, my son, I have been counting in my heart the bravest warriors of our people. There is not one of them who won his title in his sixteenth winter. My son, it is a great thing for some brave of sixteen winters to do."

Not a word had I to give in answer. I knew well the fame of my warrior father. He had earned the right of speaking such words, though even he himself was a brave only at my age. Refusing to smoke my grandmother's pipe because my heart was too much stirred by their words, and sorely troubled with a fear lest I should disappoint them, I arose to go. Drawing my blanket over my shoulders, I said, as I stepped toward the entranceway: "I go to hobble my pony. It is now late in the night."

II.

Nine winters' snows had buried deep that night when my old grandmother, together with my father and mother, designed my future with the glow of a camp fire upon it.

Yet I did not grow up the warrior, huntsman, and husband I was to have been. At the mission school I learned it was wrong to kill. Nine winters I hunted for the soft heart of Christ, and prayed for the huntsmen who chased the buffalo on the plains.

In the autumn of the tenth year I was sent back to my tribe to preach Christianity to them. With the white man's Bible in my hand, and the white man's tender heart in my breast, I returned to my own people.

Wearing a foreigner's dress, I walked, a stranger, into my father's village.

Asking my way, for I had not forgotten my native tongue, an old man led me toward the tepee where my father lay. From my old companion I learned that my father had been sick many moons. As we drew near the tepee, I heard the chanting of a medicine-man within it. At once I wished to enter in and drive from my home the sorcerer of the plains, but the old warrior checked me. "Ho, wait outside until the medicine-man leaves your father," he said. While talking he scanned me from head to feet. Then he retraced his steps toward the heart of the camping-ground.

My father's dwelling was on the outer limits of the round-faced village. With every heartthrob I grew more impatient to enter the wigwam.

While I turned the leaves of my Bible with nervous fingers, the medicine-man came forth from the dwelling and walked hurriedly away. His head and face were closely covered with the loose robe which draped his entire figure.

He was tall and large. His long strides I have never forgot. They seemed to me then the uncanny gait of eternal death. Quickly pocketing my Bible, I went into the tepee.

Upon a mat lay my father, with furrowed face and gray hair. His eyes and cheeks were sunken far into his head. His sallow skin lay thin upon his pinched nose and high cheekbones. Stooping over him, I took his fevered hand. "How, Ate?" I greeted him. A light flashed from his listless eyes and his dried lips parted. "My son!" he murmured, in a feeble voice. Then again the wave of joy and recognition receded. He closed his eyes, and his hand dropped from my open palm to the ground.

Looking about, I saw an old woman sitting with bowed head. Shaking hands with her, I recognized my mother. I sat down between my father and mother as I used to do, but I did not feel at home. The place where my old grandmother used to sit was now unoccupied. With my mother I bowed my head. Alike our throats were choked and tears were streaming from our eyes; but far apart in spirit our ideas and faiths separated us. My grief was for the soul unsaved; and I thought my mother wept to see a brave man's body broken by sickness.

Useless was my attempt to change the faith in the medicine-man to that abstract power named God. Then one day I became righteously mad with anger that the medicine-man should thus ensnare my father's soul. And when he came to chant his sacred songs I pointed toward the door and bade him go! The man's eyes glared upon me for an instant. Slowly gathering his robe about him, he turned his back upon the sick man and stepped out of our wigwam. "Ha, ha, ha! my son, I can not live without the medicine-man!" I heard my father cry when the sacred man was gone.

III.

On a bright day, when the winged seeds of the prairie-grass were flying hither and thither, I walked solemnly toward the centre of the camping-ground. My heart beat hard and irregularly at my side. Tighter I grasped the sacred book I carried under my arm. Now was the beginning of life's work.

Though I knew it would be hard, I did not once feel that failure was to be my reward. As I stepped unevenly on the rolling ground, I thought of the warriors soon to wash off their war-paints and follow me.

At length I reached the place where the people had assembled to hear me preach. In a large circle men and women sat upon the dry red grass. Within the ring I stood, with the white man's Bible in my hand. I tried to tell them of the soft heart of Christ.

In silence the vast circle of bareheaded warriors sat under an afternoon sun. At last, wiping the wet from my brow, I took my place in the ring. The hush of the assembly filled me with great hope.

I was turning my thoughts upward to the sky in gratitude, when a stir called me to earth again.

A tall, strong man arose. His loose robe hung in folds over his right shoulder. A pair of snapping black eyes fastened themselves like the poisonous fangs of a serpent upon me. He was the medicine-man. A tremor played about my heart and a chill cooled the fire in my veins.

Scornfully he pointed a long forefinger in my direction and asked:

"What loyal son is he who, returning to his father's people, wears a foreigner's dress?" He paused a moment, and then continued: "The dress of that foreigner of whom a story says he bound a native of our land, and heaping dry sticks around him, kindled a fire at his feet!" Waving his hand toward me, he exclaimed, "Here is the traitor to his people!"

I was helpless. Before the eyes of the crowd the cunning magician turned my honest heart into a vile nest of treachery. Alas! the people frowned as they looked upon me.

"Listen!" he went on. "Which one of you who have eyed the young man can see through his bosom and warn the people of the nest of young snakes hatching there? Whose ear was so acute that he caught the hissing of snakes whenever the young man opened his mouth? This one has not only proven false to you, but even to the Great Spirit who made him. He is a fool! Why do you sit here giving ear to a foolish man who could not defend his people because he fears to kill, who could not bring venison to renew the life of his sick father? With his prayers, let him drive away the enemy! With his soft heart, let him keep off starvation! We shall go elsewhere to dwell upon an untainted ground."

With this he disbanded the people. When the sun lowered in the west and the winds were quiet, the village of cone-shaped tepees was gone. The medicine-man had won the hearts of the people.

Only my father's dwelling was left to mark the fighting-ground.

IV.

From a long night at my father's bedside I came out to look upon the morning. The yellow sun hung equally between the snow-covered land and the cloudless blue sky. The light of the new day was cold. The strong breath of winter crusted the snow and fitted crystal shells over the rivers and lakes. As I stood in front of the tepee, thinking of the vast prairies which separated us from our tribe, and wondering if the high sky likewise separated the soft-hearted Son of God from us, the icy blast from the North blew through my hair and skull. My neglected hair had grown long and fell upon my neck.

My father had not risen from his bed since the day the medicine-man led the people away. Though I read from the Bible and prayed beside him upon my knees, my father would not listen. Yet I believed my prayers were not unheeded in heaven.

"Ha, ha, ha! my son," my father groaned upon the first snowfall. "My son, our food is gone. There is no one to bring me meat! My son, your soft heart has unfitted you for everything!" Then covering his face with the buffalo-robe, he said no more. Now while I stood out in that cold winter morning, I was starving. For two days I had not seen any food. But my own cold and hunger did not harass my soul as did the whining cry of the sick old man.

Stepping again into the tepee, I untied my snow-shoes, which were fastened to the tent-poles.

My poor mother, watching by the sick one, and faithfully heaping wood upon the centre fire, spoke to me:

"My son, do not fail again to bring your father meat, or he will starve to death."

"How, Ina," I answered, sorrowfully. From the tepee I started forth again to hunt food for my aged parents. All day I tracked the white level lands in vain. Nowhere, nowhere were there any other footprints but my own! In the evening of this third fast-day I came back without meat. Only a bundle of sticks for the fire I brought on my back. Dropping the wood outside, I lifted the door-flap and set one foot within the tepee.

There I grew dizzy and numb. My eyes swam in tears. Before me lay my old gray-haired father sobbing like a child. In his horny hands he clutched the buffalo-robe, and with his teeth he was gnawing off the edges. Chewing the dry stiff hair and buffalo-skin, my father's eyes sought my hands. Upon seeing them empty, he cried out:

"My son, your soft heart will let me starve before you bring me meat! Two hills eastward stand a herd of cattle. Yet you will see me die before you bring me food!"

Leaving my mother lying with covered head upon her mat, I rushed out into the night.

With a strange warmth in my heart and swiftness in my feet, I climbed over the first hill, and soon the second one. The moonlight upon the white country showed me a clear path to the white man's cattle. With my hand upon the knife in my belt, I leaned heavily against the fence while counting the herd.

Twenty in all I numbered. From among them I chose the best-fattened creature. Leaping over the fence, I plunged my knife into it.

My long knife was sharp, and my hands, no more fearful and slow, slashed off choice chunks of warm flesh. Bending under the meat I had taken for my starving father, I hurried across the prairie.

Toward home I fairly ran with the life-giving food I carried upon my back. Hardly had I climbed the second hill when I heard sounds coming after me. Faster and faster I ran with my load for my father, but the sounds were gaining upon me. I heard the clicking of snowshoes and the squeaking of the leather straps at my heels; yet I did not turn to see what pursued me, for I was intent upon reaching my father. Suddenly like thunder an angry voice shouted curses and threats into my ear! A rough hand wrenched my shoulder and took the meat from me! I stopped struggling to run. A deafening whir filled my head. The moon and stars began to move. Now the white prairie was sky, and the stars lay under my feet. Now again they were turning. At last the starry blue rose up into place. The noise in my ears was still. A great quiet filled the air. In my hand I found my long knife dripping with blood. At my feet a man's figure lay prone in blood-red snow. The horrible scene about me seemed a trick of my senses, for I could not understand it was real. Looking long upon the blood-stained snow, the load of meat for my starving father reached my recognition at last. Quickly I tossed it over my shoulder and started again homeward.

Tired and haunted I reached the door of the wigwam. Carrying the food before me, I entered with it into the tepee.

"Father, here is food!" I cried, as I dropped the meat near my mother. No answer came. Turning about, I beheld my gray-haired father dead! I saw by the unsteady firelight an old gray-haired skeleton lying rigid and stiff.

Out into the open I started, but the snow at my feet became bloody.

V.

On the day after my father's death, having led my mother to the camp of the medicine-man, I gave myself up to those who were searching for the murderer of the paleface.

They bound me hand and foot. Here in this cell I was placed four days ago.

The shrieking winter winds have followed me hither. Rattling the bars, they howl unceasingly: "Your soft heart! your soft heart will see me die before you bring me food!" Hark! something is clanking the chain on the door. It is being opened. From the dark night without a black figure crosses the threshold. * * * It is the guard. He comes to warn me of my fate. He tells me that tomorrow I must die. In his stern face I laugh aloud. I do not fear death.

Yet I wonder who shall come to welcome me in the realm of strange sight. Will the loving Jesus grant me pardon and give my soul a soothing sleep? or will my warrior father greet me and receive me as his son? Will my spirit fly upward to a happy heaven? or shall I sink into the bottomless pit, an outcast from a God of infinite love?

Soon, soon I shall know, for now I see the east is growing red. My heart is strong. My face is calm. My eyes are dry and eager for new scenes. My hands hang quietly at my side. Serene and brave, my soul awaits the men to perch me on the gallows for another flight. I go.

THE TRIAL PATH

It was an autumn night on the plain. The smoke-lapels of the cone-shaped tepee flapped gently in the breeze. From the low night sky, with its myriad fire points, a large bright star peeped in at the smoke-hole of the wigwam between its fluttering lapels, down upon two Dakotas talking in the dark. The mellow stream from the star above, a maid of twenty summers, on a bed of sweetgrass, drank in with her wakeful eyes. On the opposite side of the tepee, beyond the centre fireplace, the grandmother spread her rug. Though once she had lain down, the telling of a story has aroused her to a sitting posture.

Her eyes are tight closed. With a thin palm she strokes her wind-shorn hair.

"Yes, my grandchild, the legend says the large bright stars are wise old warriors, and the small dim ones are handsome young braves," she reiterates, in a high, tremulous voice.

"Then this one peeping in at the smoke-hole yonder is my dear old grandfather," muses the young woman, in long-drawn-out words.

Her soft rich voice floats through the darkness within the tepee, over the cold ashes heaped on the centre fire, and passes into the ear of the toothless old woman, who sits dumb in silent reverie. Thence it flies on swifter wing over many winter snows, till at last it cleaves the warm light atmosphere of her grandfather's youth. From there her grandmother made answer:

"Listen! I am young again. It is the day of your grandfather's death. The elder one, I mean, for there were two of them. They were like twins, though they were not brothers. They were friends, inseparable! All things, good and bad, they shared together, save one, which made them mad. In that heated frenzy the younger man slew his most intimate friend. He killed his elder brother, for long had their affection made them kin."

The voice of the old woman broke. Swaying her stooped shoulders to and fro as she sat upon her feet, she muttered vain exclamations beneath her breath. Her eyes, closed tight against the night, beheld behind them the light of bygone days. They saw again a rolling black cloud spread itself over the land. Her ear heard the deep rumbling of a tempest in the west. She bent low a cowering head, while angry thunder-birds shrieked across the sky. "Heyã! heyã!" (No! no!) groaned the toothless grandmother at the fury she had awakened. But the glorious peace afterward, when yellow sunshine made the people glad, now lured her memory onward through the storm.

"How fast, how loud my heart beats as I listen to the messenger's horrible tale!" she ejaculates. "From the fresh grave of the murdered man he hurried to our wigwam. Deliberately crossing his bare shins, he sat down unbidden beside my father, smoking a long-stemmed pipe. He had scarce caught his breath when, panting, he began:

"'He was an only son, and a much-adored brother.'

"With wild, suspecting eyes he glanced at me as if I were in league with the man-killer, my lover. My father, exhaling sweet-scented smoke, assented—'How.' Then interrupting the 'Eya' on the lips of the round-eyed talebearer, he asked, 'My friend, will you smoke?' He took the pipe by its red-stone bowl, and pointed the long slender stem toward the man. 'Yes, yes, my friend,' replied he, and reached out a long brown arm.

"For many heart-throbs he puffed out the blue smoke, which hung like a cloud between us. But even through the smoke-mist I saw his sharp black eyes glittering toward me. I longed to ask what doom awaited the young murderer, but dared not open my lips, lest I burst forth into screams instead. My father plied the question. Returning the pipe, the man replied: 'Oh, the chieftain and his chosen men have had counsel together. They have agreed it is not safe to allow a man-killer loose in our midst. He who kills one of our tribe is an enemy, and must suffer the fate of a foe.'

"My temples throbbed like a pair of hearts!

"While I listened, a crier passed by my father's tepee. Mounted, and swaying with his pony's steps, he proclaimed in a loud voice these words (hark! I hear them now!): "Ho-po! Give ear, all you people. A terrible deed is done. Two friends—ay, brothers in heart—have quarreled together. Now one lies buried on the hill, while the other sits, a dreaded man-killer, within his dwelling." Says our chieftain: "He who kills one of our tribe commits the offense of an enemy. As such he must be tried. Let the father of the dead man choose the mode of torture or taking of life. He has suffered livid pain, and he alone can judge how great the punishment must be to avenge his wrong." It is done.

"'Come, every one, to witness the judgment of a father upon him who was once his son's best friend. A wild pony is now lassoed. The man-killer must mount and ride the ranting beast. Stand you all in two parallel lines from the centre tepee of the bereaved family to the wigwam opposite in the great outer ring. Between you, in the wide space, is the given trial-way. From the outer circle the rider must mount and guide his pony toward the centre tepee. If, having gone the entire distance, the man-killer gains the centre tepee still sitting on the pony's back, his life is spared and pardon given. But should he fall, then he himself has chosen death.'

"The crier's words now cease. A lull holds the village breathless. Then hurrying feet tear along, swish, swish, through the tall grass. Sobbing women hasten toward the trialway. The muffled groan of the round camp-ground is unbearable. With my face hid in the folds of my blanket, I run with the crowd toward the open place in the outer circle of our village. In a moment the two long files of solemn-faced people mark the path of the public trial. Ah! I see strong men trying to lead the lassoed pony, pitching and rearing, with white foam flying from his mouth. I choke with pain as I recognize my handsome lover desolately alone, striding with set face toward the lassoed pony. 'Do not fall! Choose life and me!' I cry in my breast, but over my lips I hold my thick blanket.

"In an instant he has leaped astride the frightened beast, and the men have let go their hold. Like an arrow sprung from a strong bow, the pony, with extended nostrils, plunges halfway to the centre tepee. With all his might the rider draws the strong reins in. The pony halts with wooden legs. The rider is thrown forward by force, but does not fall. Now the maddened creature pitches, with flying heels. The line of men and women sways outward. Now it is back in place, safe from the kicking, snorting thing.

"The pony is fierce, with its large black eyes bulging out of their sockets. With humped back and nose to the ground, it leaps into the air. I shut my eyes. I can not see him fall.

"A loud shout goes up from the hoarse throats of men and women. I look. So! The wild horse is conquered. My lover dismounts at the doorway of the centre wigwam. The pony, wet with sweat and shaking with exhaustion, stands like a guilty dog at his master's side. Here at the entranceway of the tepee sit the bereaved father, mother, and sister. The old warrior father rises. Stepping forward two long strides, he grasps the hand of the murderer of his only son. Holding it so the people can see, he cries, with compassionate voice, 'My son!' A murmur of surprise sweeps like a puff of sudden wind along the lines.

"The mother, with swollen eyes, with her hair cut square with her shoulders, now rises. Hurrying to the young man, she takes his right hand. 'My son!' she greets him. But on the second word her voice shook, and she turned away in sobs.

"The young people rivet their eyes upon the young woman. She does not stir. With bowed head, she sits motionless. The old warrior speaks to her. 'Shake hands with the young brave, my little daughter. He was your brother's friend for many years. Now he must be both friend and brother to you.'

"Hereupon the girl rises. Slowly reaching out her slender hand, she cries, with twitching lips, 'My brother!' The trial ends."

"Grandmother!" exploded the girl on the bed of sweet-grass. "Is this true?"

"Tosh!" answered the grandmother, with a warmth in her voice. "It is all true. During the fifteen winters of our wedded life many ponies passed from our hands, but this little winner, Ohiyesa, was a constant member of our family. At length, on that sad day your grandfather died, Ohiyesa was killed at the grave."

Though the various groups of stars which move across the sky, marking the passing of time, told how the night was in its zenith, the old Dakota woman ventured an explanation of the burial ceremony.

"My grandchild, I have scarce ever breathed the sacred knowledge in my heart. Tonight I must tell you one of them. Surely you are old enough to understand.

"Our wise medicine-man said I did well to hasten Ohiyesa after his master. Perchance on the journey along the ghostpath your grandfather will weary, and in his heart wish for his pony. The creature, already bound on the spirit-trail, will be drawn by that subtle wish. Together master and beast will enter the next camp-ground."

The woman ceased her talking. But only the deep breathing of the girl broke the quiet, for now the night wind had lulled itself to sleep.

"Hinnu! hinnu! Asleep! I have been talking in the dark, unheard. I did wish the girl would plant in her heart this sacred tale," muttered she, in a querulous voice.

Nestling into her bed of sweet-scented grass, she dozed away into another dream. Still the guardian star in the night sky beamed compassionately down upon the little tepee on the plain.

A WARRIOR'S DAUGHTER

In the afternoon shadow of a large tepee, with red-painted smoke lapels, sat a warrior father with crossed shins. His head was so poised that his eye swept easily the vast level land to the eastern horizon line.

He was the chieftain's bravest warrior. He had won by heroic deeds the privilege of staking his wigwam within the great circle of tepees.

He was also one of the most generous gift givers to the toothless old people. For this he was entitled to the red-painted smoke lapels on his cone-shaped dwelling. He was proud of his honors. He never wearied of rehearsing nightly his own brave deeds. Though by wigwam fires he prated much of his high rank and widespread fame, his great joy was a wee black-eyed daughter of eight sturdy winters. Thus as he sat upon the soft grass, with his wife at his side, bent over her bead work, he was singing a dance song, and beat lightly the rhythm with his slender hands.

His shrewd eyes softened with pleasure as he watched the easy movements of the small body dancing on the green before him.

Tusee is taking her first dancing lesson. Her tightly-braided hair curves over both brown ears like a pair of crooked little horns which glisten in the summer sun.

With her snugly moccasined feet close together, and a wee hand at her belt to stay the long string of beads which hang from her bare neck, she bends her knees gently to the rhythm of her father's voice.

Now she ventures upon the earnest movement, slightly upward and sidewise, in a circle. At length the song drops into a closing cadence, and the little woman, clad in beaded deerskin, sits down beside the elder one. Like her mother, she sits upon her feet. In a brief moment the warrior repeats the last refrain. Again Tusee springs to her feet and dances to the swing of the few final measures.

Just as the dance was finished, an elderly man, with short, thick hair loose about his square shoulders, rode into their presence from the rear, and leaped lightly from his pony's back. Dropping the rawhide rein to the ground, he tossed himself lazily on the grass. "Hunhe, you have returned soon," said the warrior, while extending a hand to his little daughter.

Quickly the child ran to her father's side and cuddled close to him, while he tenderly placed a strong arm about her. Both father and child, eyeing the figure on the grass, waited to hear the man's report.

"It is true," began the man, with a stranger's accent. "This is the night of the dance."

"Hunha!" muttered the warrior with some surprise.

Propping himself upon his elbows, the man raised his face. His features were of the Southern type. From an enemy's camp he was taken captive long years ago by Tusee's father. But the unusual qualities of the slave had won the Sioux warrior's heart, and for the last three winters the man had had his freedom. He was made real man again. His hair was allowed to grow. However, he himself had chosen to stay in the warrior's family.

"Hunha!" again ejaculated the warrior father. Then turning to his little daughter, he asked, "Tusee, do you hear that?"

"Yes, father, and I am going to dance tonight!"

With these words she bounded out of his arm and frolicked about in glee. Hereupon the proud mother's voice rang out in a chiding laugh.

"My child, in honor of your first dance your father must give a generous gift. His ponies are wild, and roam beyond the great hill. Pray, what has he fit to offer?" she questioned, the pair of puzzled eyes fixed upon her.

"A pony from the herd, mother, a fleet-footed pony from the herd!" Tusee shouted with sudden inspiration.

Pointing a small forefinger toward the man lying on the grass, she cried, "Uncle, you will go after the pony tomorrow!" And pleased with her solution of the problem, she skipped wildly about. Her childish faith in her elders was not conditioned by a knowledge of human limitations, but thought all things possible to grown-ups.

"Hähob!" exclaimed the mother, with a rising inflection, implying by the expletive that her child's buoyant spirit be not weighted with a denial.

Quickly to the hard request the man replied, "How! I go if Tusee tells me so!"

This delighted the little one, whose black eyes brimmed over with light. Standing in front of the strong man, she clapped her small, brown hands with joy.

"That makes me glad! My heart is good! Go, uncle, and bring a handsome pony!" she cried. In an instant she would have frisked away, but an impulse held her tilting where she stood. In the man's own tongue, for he had taught her many words and phrases, she exploded, "Thank you, good uncle, thank you!" then tore away from sheer excess of glee.

The proud warrior father, smiling and narrowing his eyes, muttered approval, "Howo! Hechetu!"

Like her mother, Tusee has finely pencilled eyebrows and slightly extended nostrils; but in her sturdiness of form she resembles her father.

A loyal daughter, she sits within her tepee making beaded deerskins for her father, while he longs to stave off her every suitor as all unworthy of his old heart's pride. But Tusee is not alone in her dwelling. Near the entrance-way a young brave is half reclining on a mat. In silence he watches the petals of a wild rose growing on the soft buckskin. Quickly the young woman slips the beads on the silvery sinew thread, and works them into the pretty flower design. Finally, in a low, deep voice, the young man begins:

"The sun is far past the zenith. It is now only a man's height above the western edge of land. I hurried hither to tell you tomorrow I join the war party."

He pauses for reply, but the maid's head drops lower over her deerskin, and her lips are more firmly drawn together. He continues:

"Last night in the moonlight I met your warrior father. He seemed to know I had just stepped forth from your tepee. I fear he did not like it, for though I greeted him, he was silent. I halted in his pathway. With what boldness I dared, while my heart was beating hard and fast, I asked him for his only daughter.

"Drawing himself erect to his tallest height, and gathering his loose robe more closely about his proud figure, he flashed a pair of piercing eyes upon me.

"'Young man,' said he, with a cold, slow voice that chilled me to the marrow of my bones, 'hear me. Naught but an enemy's scalp-lock, plucked fresh with your own hand, will buy Tusee for your wife.' Then he turned on his heel and stalked away."

Tusee thrusts her work aside. With earnest eyes she scans her lover's face.

"My father's heart is really kind. He would know if you are brave and true," murmured the daughter, who wished no ill-will between her two loved ones.

Then rising to go, the youth holds out a right hand. "Grasp my hand once firmly before I go, Hoye. Pray tell me, will you wait and watch for my return?"

Tusee only nods assent, for mere words are vain.

At early dawn the round camp-ground awakes into song. Men and women sing of bravery and of triumph. They inspire the swelling breasts of the painted warriors mounted on prancing ponies bedecked with the green branches of trees.

Riding slowly around the great ring of cone-shaped tepees, here and there, a loud-singing warrior swears to avenge a former wrong, and thrusts a bare brown arm against the purple east, calling the Great Spirit to hear his vow. All having made the circuit, the singing war party gallops away southward.

Astride their ponies laden with food and deerskins, brave elderly women follow after their warriors. Among the foremost rides a young woman in elaborately beaded buckskin dress. Proudly mounted, she curbs with the single rawhide loop a wild-eyed pony.

It is Tusee on her father's warhorse. Thus the war party of Indian men and their faithful women vanish beyond the southern skyline.

A day's journey brings them very near the enemy's borderland. Nightfall finds a pair of twin tepees nestled in a deep ravine. Within one lounge the painted warriors, smoking their pipes and telling weird stories by the firelight, while in the other watchful women crouch uneasily about their center fire.

By the first gray light in the east the tepees are banished. They are gone. The warriors are in the enemy's camp, breaking dreams with their tomahawks. The women are hid away in secret places in the long thicketed ravine.

The day is far spent, the red sun is low over the west.

At length straggling warriors return, one by one, to the deep hollow. In the twilight they number their men. Three are missing. Of these absent ones two are dead; but the third one, a young man, is a captive to the foe.

"He-he!" lament the warriors, taking food in haste.

In silence each woman, with long strides, hurries to and fro, tying large bundles on her pony's back. Under cover of night the war party must hasten homeward. Motionless, with bowed head, sits a woman in her hiding-place. She grieves for her lover.

In bitterness of spirit she hears the warriors' murmuring words. With set teeth she plans to cheat the hated enemy of their captive. In the meanwhile low signals are given, and the war party, unaware of Tusee's absence, steal quietly away. The soft thud of pony-hoofs grows fainter and fainter. The gradual hush of the empty ravine whirrs noisily in the ear of the young woman. Alert for any sound of footfalls nigh, she holds her breath to listen. Her right hand rests on a long knife in her belt. Ah, yes, she knows where her pony is hid, but not yet has she need of him. Satisfied that no danger is nigh, she prowls forth from her place of hiding. With a panther's tread and pace she climbs the high ridge beyond the low ravine. From thence she spies the enemy's camp-fires.

Rooted to the barren bluff the slender woman's figure stands on the pinnacle of night, outlined against a starry sky. The cool night breeze wafts to her burning ear snatches of song and drum. With desperate hate she bites her teeth.

Tusee beckons the stars to witness. With impassioned voice and uplifted face she pleads:

"Great Spirit, speed me to my lover's rescue! Give me swift cunning for a weapon this night! All-powerful Spirit, grant me my warrior-father's heart, strong to slay a foe and mighty to save a friend!"

In the midst of the enemy's camp-ground, underneath a temporary dance-house, are men and women in gala-day dress. It is late in the night, but the merry warriors bend and bow their nude, painted bodies before a bright center fire. To the lusty men's voices and the rhythmic throbbing drum, they leap and rebound with feathered headgears waving.

Women with red-painted cheeks and long, braided hair sit in a large half-circle against the willow railing. They, too, join in the singing, and rise to dance with their victorious warriors.

Amid this circular dance arena stands a prisoner bound to a post, haggard with shame and sorrow. He hangs his disheveled head.

He stares with unseeing eyes upon the bare earth at his feet. With jeers and smirking faces the dancers mock the Dakota captive. Rowdy braves and small boys hoot and yell in derision.

Silent among the noisy mob, a tall woman, leaning both elbows on the round willow railing, peers into the lighted arena. The dancing center fire shines bright into her handsome face, intensifying the night in her dark eyes. It breaks into myriad points upon her beaded dress. Unmindful of the surging throng jostling her at either side, she glares in upon the hateful, scoffing men. Suddenly she turns her head. Tittering maids whisper near her ear:

"There! There! See him now, sneering in the captive's face. 'Tis he who sprang upon the young man and dragged him by his long hair to yonder post. See! He is handsome! How gracefully he dances!"

The silent young woman looks toward the bound captive. She sees a warrior, scarce older than the captive, flourishing a tomahawk in the Dakota's face. A burning rage darts forth from her eyes and brands him for a victim of revenge. Her heart mutters within her breast, "Come, I wish to meet you, vile foe, who captured my lover and tortures him now with a living death."

Here the singers hush their voices, and the dancers scatter to their various resting-places along the willow ring. The victor gives a reluctant last twirl of his tomahawk, then, like the others, he leaves the center ground. With head and shoulders swaying from side to side, he carries a high-pointing chin toward the willow railing. Sitting down upon the ground with crossed legs, he fans himself with an outspread turkey wing.

Now and then he stops his haughty blinking to peep out of the corners of his eyes. He hears some one clearing her throat gently. It is unmistakably for his ear. The wing-fan swings irregularly to and fro. At length he turns a proud face over a bare shoulder and beholds a handsome woman smiling.

"Ah, she would speak to a hero!" thumps his heart wildly.

The singers raise their voices in unison. The music is irresistible. Again lunges the victor into the open arena. Again he leers into the captive's face. At every interval between the songs he returns to his resting-place. Here the young woman awaits him. As he approaches she smiles boldly into his eyes. He is pleased with her face and her smile.

Waving his wing-fan spasmodically in front of his face, he sits with his ears pricked up. He catches a low whisper. A hand taps him lightly on the shoulder. The handsome woman speaks to him in his own tongue. "Come out into the night. I wish to tell you who I am."

He must know what sweet words of praise the handsome woman has for him. With both hands he spreads the meshes of the loosely woven willows, and crawls out unnoticed into the dark.

Before him stands the young woman. Beckoning him with a slender hand, she steps backward, away from the light and the restless throng of onlookers. He follows with impatient strides. She quickens her pace. He lengthens his strides. Then suddenly the woman turns from him and darts away with amazing speed. Clinching his fists and biting his lower lip, the young man runs after the fleeing woman. In his maddened pursuit he forgets the dance arena.

Beside a cluster of low bushes the woman halts. The young man, panting for breath and plunging headlong forward, whispers loud, "Pray tell me, are you a woman or an evil spirit to lure me away?"

Turning on heels firmly planted in the earth, the woman gives a wild spring forward, like a panther for its prey. In a husky voice she hissed between her teeth, "I am a Dakota woman!"

From her unerring long knife the enemy falls heavily at her feet. The Great Spirit heard Tusee's prayer on the hilltop. He gave her a warrior's strong heart to lessen the foe by one.

A bent old woman's figure, with a bundle like a grandchild slung on her back, walks round and round the dance-house. The wearied onlookers are leaving in twos and threes. The tired dancers creep out of the willow railing, and some go out at the entrance way, till the singers, too, rise from the drum and are trudging drowsily homeward. Within the arena the center fire lies broken in red embers. The night no longer lingers about the willow railing, but, hovering into the dance-house, covers here and there a snoring man whom sleep has overpowered where he sat.

The captive in his tight-binding rawhide ropes hangs in hopeless despair. Close about him the gloom of night is slowly crouching. Yet the last red, crackling embers cast a faint light upon his long black hair, and, shining through the thick mats, caress his wan face with undying hope.

Still about the dance-house the old woman prowls. Now the embers are gray with ashes.

The old bent woman appears at the entrance way. With a cautious, groping foot she enters. Whispering between her teeth a lullaby for her sleeping child in her blanket, she searches for something forgotten.

Noisily snored the dreaming men in the darkest parts. As the lisping old woman draws nigh, the captive again opens his eyes.

A forefinger she presses to her lip. The young man arouses himself from his stupor. His senses belie him. Before his wide-open eyes the old bent figure straightens into its youthful stature. Tusee herself is beside him. With a stroke upward and downward she severs the cruel cords with her sharp blade. Dropping her blanket from her shoulders, so that it hangs from her girdled waist like a skirt, she shakes the large bundle into a light shawl for her lover. Quickly she spreads it over his bare back.

"Come!" she whispers, and turns to go; but the young man, numb and helpless, staggers nigh to falling.

The sight of his weakness makes her strong. A mighty power thrills her body. Stooping beneath his outstretched arms grasping at the air for support, Tusee lifts him upon her broad shoulders. With half-running, triumphant steps she carries him away into the open night.

A DREAM OF HER GRANDFATHER

Her grandfather was a Dakota "medicine man." Among the Indians of his day he was widely known for his successful healing work. He was one of the leading men of the tribe and came to Washington, D.C., with one of the first delegations relative to affairs concerning the Indian people and the United States government.

His was the first band of the Great Sioux Nation to make treaties with the government in the hope of bringing about an amicable arrangement between the red and white Americans. The journey to the nation's capital was made almost entirely on pony-back, there being no railroads, and the Sioux delegation was beset with many hardships on the trail. His visit to Washington, in behalf of peace among men, proved to be his last earthly mission. From a sudden illness, he died and was buried here.

When his small granddaughter grew up she learned the white man's tongue, and followed in the footsteps of her grandfather to the very seat of government to carry on his humanitarian work. Though her days were filled with problems for welfare work among her people, she had a strange dream one night during her stay in Washington. The dream was this: Returning from an afternoon out, she found a large cedar chest had been delivered to her home in her absence. She sniffed the sweet perfume of the red wood, which reminded her of the breath of the forest,—and admired the box so neatly made, without trimmings. It looked so clean, strong and durable in its native genuineness. With elation, she took the tag in her hand and read her name aloud. "Who sent me this cedar chest?" she asked, and was told it came from her grandfather.

Wondering what gift it could be her grandfather wished now to confer upon her, wholly disregarding his death years ago, she was all eagerness to open the mystery chest.

She remembered her childhood days and the stories she loved to hear about the unusual powers of her grandfather,—recalled how she, the wee girl, had coveted the medicine bags, beaded and embroidered in porcupine quills, in symbols designed by the great "medicine man," her grandfather. Well did she remember her merited rebuke that such things were never made for relics. Treasures came in due time to those ready to receive them.

In great expectancy, she lifted the heavy lid of the cedar chest. "Oh!" she exclaimed, with a note of disappointment, seeing no beaded Indian regalia or trinkets. "Why does my grandfather send such a light gift in a heavy, large box?" She was mystified and much perplexed.

The gift was a fantastic thing, of texture far more delicate than a spider's filmy web. It was a vision! A picture of an Indian camp, not painted on canvas nor yet written. It was dream-stuff, suspended in the thin air, filling the inclosure of the cedar wood container. As she looked upon it, the picture grew more and more real, exceeding the proportions of the chest. It was all so illusive a breath might have blown it away; yet there it was, real as life,—a circular camp of white cone-shaped tepees, astir with Indian people. The village crier, with flowing head-dress of eagle plumes, mounted on a prancing white pony, rode within the arena. Indian men, women and children stopped in groups and clusters, while bright painted faces peered out of tepee doors, to listen to the chieftain's crier.

At this point, she, too, heard the full melodious voice. She heard distinctly the Dakota words he proclaimed to the people. "Be glad! Rejoice! Look up, and see the new day dawning! Help is near! Hear me, every one."

She caught the glad tidings and was thrilled with new hope for her people.

THE WIDESPREAD ENIGMA CONCERNING BLUE-STAR WOMAN

It was summer on the western plains. Fields of golden sunflowers facing eastward, greeted the rising sun. Blue-Star Woman, with windshorn braids of white hair over each ear, sat in the shade of her log hut before an open fire. Lonely but unmolested she dwelt here like the ground squirrel that took its abode nearby,—both through the easy tolerance of the land owner. The Indian woman held a skillet over the burning embers. A large round cake, with long slashes in its center, was baking and crowding the capacity of the frying pan.

In deep abstraction Blue-Star Woman prepared her morning meal. "Who am I?" had become the obsessing riddle of her life. She was no longer a young woman, being in her fifty-third year. In the eyes of the white man's law, it was required of her to give proof of her membership in the Sioux tribe. The unwritten law of heart prompted her naturally to say, "I am a being. I am Blue-Star Woman. A piece of earth is my birthright."

It was taught for reasons now forgot that an Indian should never pronounce his or her name in answer to any inquiry. It was probably a means of protection in the days of black magic. Be this as it may, Blue-Star Woman lived in times when this teaching was disregarded. It gained her nothing, however, to pronounce her name to the government official to whom she applied for her share of tribal land. His persistent question was always, "Who were your parents?"

Blue-Star Woman was left an orphan at a tender age. She did not remember them. They were long gone to the spirit-land,—and she could not understand why they should be recalled to earth on her account. It was another one of the old, old teachings of her race that the names of the dead should not be idly spoken. It had become a sacrilege to mention carelessly the name of any departed one, especially in matters of disputes over worldy possessions. The unfortunate circumstances of her early childhood, together with the lack of written records of a roving people, placed a formidable barrier between her and her heritage. The fact was events of far greater importance to the tribe than her reincarnation had passed unrecorded in books. The verbal reports of the old-time men and women of the tribe were varied,—some were actually contradictory. Blue-Star Woman was unable to find even a twig of her family tree.

She sharpened one end of a long stick and with it speared the fried bread when it was browned. Heedless of the hot bread's "Tsing!" in a high treble as it was lifted from the fire, she added it to the six others which had preceded it. It had been many a moon since she had had a meal of fried bread, for she was too poor to buy at any one time all the necessary ingredients, particularly the fat in which to fry it. During the breadmaking, the smoke-blackened coffeepot boiled over. The aroma of freshly made coffee smote her nostrils and roused her from the tantalizing memories.

The day before, friendly spirits, the unseen ones, had guided her aimless footsteps to her Indian neighbor's house. No sooner had she entered than she saw on the table some grocery bundles. "Iye-que, fortunate one!" she exclaimed as she took the straight-backed chair offered her. At once the Indian hostess untied the bundles and measured out a cupful of green coffee beans and a pound of lard. She gave them to Blue-Star Woman, saying, "I want to share my good fortune. Take these home with you." Thus it was that Blue-Star Woman had come into unexpected possession of the materials which now contributed richly to her breakfast.

The generosity of her friend had often saved her from starvation. Generosity is said to be a fault of Indian people, but neither the Pilgrim Fathers nor Blue-Star Woman ever held it seriously against them. Blue-Star Woman was even grateful for this gift of food. She was fond of coffee,—that black drink brought hither by those daring voyagers of long ago. The coffee habit was one of the signs of her progress in the white man's civilization, also had she emerged from the tepee into a log hut, another achievement. She had learned to read the primer and to write her name. Little Blue-Star attended school unhindered by a fond mother's fears that a foreign teacher might not spare the rod with her darling.

Blue-Star Woman was her individual name. For untold ages the Indian race had not used family names. A new-born child was given a brand-new name. Blue-Star Woman was proud to write her name for which she would not be required to substitute another's upon her marriage, as is the custom of civilized peoples.

"The times are changed now," she muttered under her breath. "My individual name seems to mean nothing." Looking out into space, she saw the nodding sunflowers, and they acquiesced with her. Their drying leaves reminded her of the near approach of autumn. Then soon, very soon, the ice would freeze along the banks of the muddy river. The day of the first ice was her birthday. She would be fifty-four winters old. How futile had been all these winters to secure her a share in tribal lands. A weary smile flickered across her face as she sat there on the ground like a bronze figure of patience and long-suffering.

The breadmaking was finished. The skillet was set aside to cool. She poured the appetizing coffee into her tin cup. With fried bread and black coffee she regaled herself. Again her mind reverted to her riddle. "The missionary preacher said he could not explain the white man's law to me. He who reads daily from the Holy Bible, which he tells me is God's book, cannot understand mere man's laws. This also puzzles me," thought she to herself. "Once a wise leader of our people, addressing a president of this country, said: 'I am a man. You are another. The Great Spirit is our witness!' This is simple and easy to understand, but the times are changed. The white man's laws are strange."

Blue-Star Woman broke off a piece of fried bread between a thumb and forefinger. She ate it hungrily, and sipped from her cup of fragrant coffee. "I do not understand the white man's law. It's like walking in the dark. In this darkness, I am growing fearful of everything."

Oblivious to the world, she had not heard the footfall of two Indian men who now stood before her.

Their short-cropped hair looked blue-black in contrast to the faded civilian clothes they wore. Their white man's shoes were rusty and unpolished. To the unconventional eyes of the old Indian woman, their celluloid collars appeared like shining marks of civilization. Blue-Star Woman looked up from the lap of mother earth without rising. "Hinnu, hinnu!" she ejaculated in undisguised surprise. "Pray, who are these would-be white men?" she inquired.

In one voice and by an assumed relationship the two Indian men addressed her. "Aunt, I shake hands with you." Again Blue-Star Woman remarked, "Oh, indeed! these near white men speak my native tongue and shake hands according to our custom." Did she guess the truth, she would have known they were simply deluded mortals, deceiving others and themselves most of all. Boisterously laughing and making conversation, they each in turn gripped her withered hand.

Like a sudden flurry of wind, tossing loose ends of things, they broke into her quiet morning hour and threw her groping thoughts into greater chaos. Masking their real errand with long-drawn faces, they feigned a concern for her welfare only. "We come to ask how you are living. We heard you were slowly starving to death. We heard you are one of those Indians who have been cheated out of their share in tribal lands by the government officials."

Blue-Star Woman became intensely interested.

"You see we are educated in the white man's ways," they said with protruding chests. One unconsciously thrust his thumbs into the arm-holes of his ill-fitting coat and strutted about in his pride. "We can help you get your land. We want to help our aunt. All old people like you ought to be helped before the younger ones. The old will die soon, and they may never get the benefit of their land unless some one like us helps them to get their rights, without further delay."

Blue-Star Woman listened attentively.

Motioning to the mats she spread upon the ground, she said: "Be seated, my nephews." She accepted the relationship assumed for the occasion. "I will give you some breakfast." Quickly she set before them a generous helping of fried bread and cups of coffee. Resuming her own meal, she continued, "You are wonderfully kind. It is true, my nephews, that I have grown old trying to secure my share of land. It may not be long till I shall pass under the sod."

The two men responded with "How, how," which meant, "Go on with your story. We are all ears." Blue-Star Woman had not yet detected any particular sharpness about their ears, but by an impulse she looked up into their faces and scrutinized them. They were busily engaged in eating. Their eyes were fast upon the food on the mat in front of their crossed shins. Inwardly she made a passing observation how, like ravenous wolves, her nephews devoured their food. Coyotes in midwinter could not have been more starved. Without comment she offered them the remaining fried cakes, and between them they took it all. She offered the second helping of coffee, which they accepted without hesitancy. Filling their cups, she placed her empty coffeepot on the dead ashes.

To them she rehearsed her many hardships. It had become a habit now to tell her long story of disappointments with all its petty details. It was only another instance of good intentions gone awry. It was a paradox upon a land of prophecy that its path to future glory be stained with the blood of its aborigines. Incongruous as it is, the two nephews, with their white associates, were glad of a condition so profitable to them. Their solicitation for Blue-Star Woman was not at all altruistic. They thrived in their grafting business. They and their occupation were the by-product of an unwieldly bureaucracy over the nation's wards.

"Dear aunt, you failed to establish the facts of your identity," they told her. Hereupon Blue-Star Woman's countenance fell. It was ever the same old words. It was the old song of the government official she loathed to hear. The next remark restored her courage. "If any one can discover evidence, it's us! I tell you, aunt, we'll fix it all up for you." It was a great relief to the old Indian woman to be thus unburdened of her riddle, with a prospect of possessing land. "There is one thing you will have to do,—that is, to pay us half of your land and money when you get them." Here was a pause, and Blue-Star Woman answered slowly, "Y-e-s," in an uncertain frame of mind.

The shrewd schemers noted her behavior. "Wouldn't you rather have a half of a crust of bread than none at all?" they asked. She was duly impressed with the force of their argument. In her heart she agreed, "A little something to eat is better than nothing!" The two men talked in regular relays. The flow of smooth words was continuous and so much like purring that all the woman's suspicions were put soundly to sleep. "Look here, aunt, you know very well that prairie fire is met with a back-fire." Blue-Star Woman, recalling her experiences in fire-fighting, quickly responded, "Yes, oh, yes."

"In just the same way, we fight crooks with crooks. We have clever white lawyers working with us. They are the back-fire." Then, as if remembering some particular incident, they both laughed aloud and said, "Yes, and sometimes they use us as the back-fire! We trade fifty-fifty."

Blue-Star Woman sat with her chin in the palm of one hand with elbow resting in the other. She rocked herself slightly forward and backward. At length she answered, "Yes, I will pay you half of my share in tribal land and money when I get them. In bygone days, brave young men of the order of the White-Horse-Riders sought out the aged, the poor, the widows and orphans to aid them, but they did their good work without pay. The White-Horse-Riders are gone. The times are changed. I am a poor old Indian woman. I need warm clothing before winter begins to blow its icicles through us. I need fire wood. I need food. As you have said, a little help is better than none."

Hereupon the two pretenders scored another success.

They rose to their feet. They had eaten up all the fried bread and drained the coffeepot. They shook hands with Blue-Star Woman and departed. In the quiet that followed their departure she sat munching her small piece of bread, which, by a lucky chance, she had taken on her plate before the hungry wolves had come. Very slowly she ate the fragment of fried bread as if to increase it by diligent mastication. A self-condemning sense of guilt disturbed her. In her dire need she had become involved with tricksters. Her nephews laughingly told her, "We use crooks, and crooks use us in the skirmish over Indian lands."

The friendly shade of the house shrank away from her and hid itself under the narrow eaves of the dirt covered roof. She shrugged her shoulders. The sun high in the sky had witnessed the affair and now glared down upon her white head. Gathering upon her arm the mats and cooking utensils, she hobbled into her log hut.

Under the brooding wilderness silence, on the Sioux Indian Reservation, the superintendent summoned together the leading

Indian men of the tribe. He read a letter which he had received from headquarters in Washington, D.C. It announced the enrollment of Blue-Star Woman on their tribal roll of members and the approval of allotting land to her.

It came as a great shock to the tribesmen. Without their knowledge and consent their property was given to a strange woman. They protested in vain. The superintendent said, "I received this letter from Washington. I have read it to you for your information. I have fulfilled my duty. I can do no more." With these fateful words he dismissed the assembly.

Heavy hearted, Chief High Flier returned to his dwelling. Smoking his long-stemmed pipe he pondered over the case of Blue-Star Woman. The Indian's guardian had got into a way of usurping autocratic power in disposing of the wards' property. It was growing intolerable. "No doubt this Indian woman is entitled to allotment, but where? Certainly not here," he thought to himself.

Laying down his pipe, he called his little granddaughter from her play, "You are my interpreter and scribe," he said. "Bring your paper and pencil." A letter was written in the child's sprawling hand, and signed by the old chieftain. It read:

> "My Friend:
>
> "I make letter to you. My heart is sad. Washington give my tribe's land to a woman called Blue-Star. We do not know her. We were not asked to give land, but our land is taken from us to give to another Indian. This is not right. Lots of little children of my tribe have no land. Why this strange woman get our land which belongs to our children? Go to Washington and ask if our treaties tell him to give our property away without asking us. Tell him I thought we made good treaties on paper, but now our children cry for food. We are too poor. We cannot give even to our own little children. Washington is very rich.

Washington now owns our country. If he wants to help this poor Indian woman, Blue-Star, let him give her some of his land and his money. This is all I will say until you answer me. I shake hands with you with my heart. The Great Spirit hears my words. They are true.

"Your friend,
"CHIEF HIGH FLIER.
"X (his mark)."

The letter was addressed to a prominent American woman. A stamp was carefully placed on the envelope.

Early the next morning, before the dew was off the grass, the chieftain's riding pony was caught from the pasture and brought to his log house. It was saddled and bridled by a younger man, his son with whom he made his home. The old chieftain came out, carrying in one hand his long-stemmed pipe and tobacco pouch. His blanket was loosely girdled about his waist. Tightly holding the saddle horn, he placed a moccasined foot carefully into the stirrup and pulled himself up awkwardly into the saddle, muttering to himself, "Alas, I can no more leap into my saddle. I now must crawl about in my helplessness." He was past eighty years of age, and no longer agile.

He set upon his ten-mile trip to the only post office for hundreds of miles around. In his shirt pocket, he carried the letter destined, in due season, to reach the heart of American people. His pony, grown old in service, jogged along the dusty road. Memories of other days thronged the wayside, and for the lonely rider transformed all the country. Those days were gone when the Indian youths were taught to be truthful,—to be merciful to the poor. Those days were gone when moral cleanliness was a chief virtue; when public feasts were given in honor of the virtuous girls and young men of the tribe.

Untold mischief is now possible through these broken ancient laws. The younger generation were not being properly trained in the high virtues. A slowly starving race was growing mad, and the pitifully weak sold their lands for a pot of porridge.

"He, he, he! He, he, he!" he lamented. "Small Voice Woman, my own relative is being represented as the mother of this strange Blue-Star—the papers were made by two young Indian men who have learned the white man's ways. Why must I be forced to accept the mischief of children? My memory is clear. My reputation for veracity is well known.

"Small Voice Woman lived in my house until her death. She had only one child and it was a *boy*!" He held his hand over this thumping heart, and was reminded of the letter in his pocket. "This letter,—what will happen when it reaches my good friend?" he asked himself. The chieftain rubbed his dim eyes and groaned, "If only my good friend knew the folly of turning my letter into the hands of bureaucrats! In face of repeated defeat, I am daring once more to send this one letter." An inner voice said in his ear, "And this one letter will share the same fate of the other letters."

Startled by the unexpected voice, he jerked upon the bridle reins and brought the drowsy pony to a sudden halt. There was no one near. He found himself a mile from the post office, for the cluster of government buildings, where lived the superintendent, were now in plain sight. His thin frame shook with emotion. He could not go there with his letter.

He dismounted from his pony. His quavering voice chanted a bravery song as he gathered dry grasses and the dead stalks of last year's sunflowers. He built a fire, and crying aloud, for his sorrow was greater than he could bear, he cast the letter into the flames. The fire consumed it. He sent his message on the wings of fire and he believed she would get it. He yet trusted that help would come to his people before it was too late. The pony tossed his head in a readiness to go. He knew he was on the return trip and he was glad to travel.

The wind which blew so gently at dawn was now increased into a gale as the sun approached the zenith. The chieftain, on his way home, sensed a coming storm. He looked upward to the sky and around in every direction. Behind him, in the distance, he saw a cloud of dust. He saw several horsemen whipping their ponies and riding at great speed. Occasionally he heard their shouts, as if calling after some one. He slackened his pony's pace and frequently looked over his shoulder to see who the riders were advancing in hot haste upon him. He was growing curious. In a short time the riders surrounded him. On their coats shone brass buttons, and on their hats were gold cords and tassels. They were Indian police.

"Wan!" he exclaimed, finding himself the object of their chase. It was their foolish ilk who had murdered the great leader, Sitting Bull. "Pray, what is the joke? Why do young men surround an old man quietly riding home?"

"Uncle," said the spokesman, "we are hirelings, as you know. We are sent by the government superintendent to arrest you and take you back with us. The superintendent says you are one of the bad Indians, singing war songs and opposing the government all the time; this morning you were seen trying to set fire to the government agency."

"Hunhunhe!" replied the old chief, placing the palm of his hand over his mouth agape in astonishment. "All this is unbelievable!"

The policeman took hold of the pony's bridle and turned the reluctant little beast around. They led it back with them and the old chieftain set unresisting in the saddle. High Flier was taken before the superintendent, who charged him with setting fires to destroy government buildings and found him guilty. Thus Chief

High Flier was sent to jail. He had already suffered much during his life. He was the voiceless man of America. And now in his old age he was cast into prison. The chagrin of it all, together with his utter helplessness to defend his own or his people's human rights, weighed heavily upon his spirit.

The foul air of the dingy cell nauseated him who loved the open. He sat wearily down upon the tattered mattress, which lay on the rough board floor. He drew his robe closely about his tall figure, holding it partially over his face, his hands covered within the folds. In profound gloom the gray-haired prisoner sat there, without a stir for long hours and knew not when the day ended and night began. He sat buried in his desperation. His eyes were closed, but he could not sleep. Bread and water in tin receptacles set upon the floor beside him untouched. He was not hungry. Venturesome mice crept out upon the floor and scampered in the dim starlight streaming through the iron bars of the cell window. They squeaked as they dared each other to run across his moccasined feet, but the chieftain neither saw nor heard them.

A terrific struggle was waged within his being. He fought as he never fought before. Tenaciously he hung upon hope for the day of salvation—that hope hoary with age. Defying all odds against him, he refused to surrender faith in good people.

Underneath his blanket, wrapped so closely about him, stole a luminous light. Before his stricken consciousness appeared a vision. Lo, his good friend, the American woman to whom he had sent his messages by fire, now stood there a legion! A vast multitude of women, with uplifted hands, gazed upon a huge stone image. Their upturned faces were eager and very earnest. The stone figure was that of a woman upon the brink of the Great Waters, facing eastward. The myriad living hands remained uplifted till the stone woman began to show signs of life. Very majestically she turned around, and, lo, she smiled upon this great galaxy of American women. She was the Statue of Liberty! It was she, who, though representing human liberty, formerly turned her back upon the American aborigine. Her face was aglow with compassion. Her eyes swept across the outspread continent of America, the home of the red man.

At this moment her torch flamed brighter and whiter till its radiance reached into the obscure and remote places of the land. Her light of liberty penetrated Indian reservations. A loud shout of joy rose up from the Indians of the earth, everywhere!

All too soon the picture was gone. Chief High Flier awoke. He lay prostrate on the floor where during the night he had fallen. He rose and took his seat again upon the mattress. Another day was ushered into his life. In his heart lay the secret vision of hope born in the midnight of his sorrows. It enabled him to serve his jail sentence with a mute dignity which baffled those who saw him.

Finally came the day of his release. There was rejoicing over all the land. The desolate hills that harbored wailing voices nightly now were hushed and still. Only gladness filled the air. A crowd gathered around the jail to greet the chieftain. His son stood at the entrance way, while the guard unlocked the prison door. Serenely quiet, the old Indian chief stepped forth. An unseen stone in his path caused him to stumble slightly, but his son grasped him by the hand and steadied his tottering steps. He led him to a heavy lumber wagon drawn by a small pony team which he had brought to take him home. The people thronged about him—hundreds shook hands with him and went away singing native songs of joy for the safe return to them of their absent one.

Among the happy people came Blue-Star Woman's two nephews. Each shook the chieftain's hand. One of them held out an ink pad saying, "We are glad we were able to get you out of jail. We have great influence with the Indian Bureau in Washington, D.C. When you need help, let us know. Here press your thumb in this pad." His companion took from his pocket a document prepared for the old chief's signature, and held it on the wagon wheel for the thumb mark. The chieftain was taken by surprise. He looked into his son's eyes to know the meaning of these two men. "It is our agreement," he explained to his old father. "I pledged to pay them half of your land if they got you out of jail."

The old chieftain sighed, but made no comment. Words were vain. He pressed his indelible thumb mark, his signature it was, upon the deed, and drove home with his son.

AMERICA'S INDIAN PROBLEM

AMERICA'S INDIAN PROBLEM

The hospitality of the American aborigine, it is told, saved the early settlers from starvation during the first bleak winters. In commemoration of having been so well received, Newport erected "a cross as a sign of English dominion." With sweet words he quieted the suspicions of Chief Powhatan, his friend. He "told him that the arms (of the cross) represented Powhatan and himself, and the middle their united league."

DeSoto and his Spaniards were graciously received by the Indian Princess Cofachiqui in the South. While on a sight-seeing tour they entered the ancestral tombs of those Indians. DeSoto "dipped into the pearls and gave his two joined hands full to each cavalier to make rosaries of, he said, to say prayers for their sins on. We imagine if their prayers were in proportion to their sins they must have spent the most of their time at their devotions."

It was in this fashion that the old world snatched away the fee in the land of the new. It was in this fashion that America was divided between the powers of Europe and the aborigines were dispossessed of their country. The barbaric rule of might from which the paleface had fled hither for refuge caught up with him again, and in the melee the hospitable native suffered "legal disability."

History tells that it was from the English and the Spanish our government inherited its legal victims, the American Indians, whom to this day we hold as wards and not as citizens of their own freedom loving land. A long century of dishonor followed this inheritance of somebody's loot. Now the time is at hand when the American Indian shall have his day in court through the help of the women of America. The stain upon America's fair name is to be removed, and the remnant of the Indian nation, suffering from malnutrition, is to number among the invited invisible guests at your dinner tables.

In this undertaking there must be cooperation of head, heart and hand. We serve both our own government and a voiceless people within our midst. We would open the door of American opportunity to the red man and encourage him to find his rightful place in our American life. We would remove the barriers that hinder his normal development.

Wardship is no substitute for American citizenship, therefore we seek his enfranchisement. The many treaties made in good faith with the Indian by our government we would like to see equitably settled. By a constructive program we hope to do away with the "piecemeal legislation" affecting Indians here and there which has proven an exceedingly expensive and disappointing method.

Do you know what *your* Bureau of Indian Affairs, in Washington, D.C., really is? How it is organized and how it deals with wards of the nation? This is our first study. Let us be informed of facts and then we may formulate our opinions. In the remaining space allowed me I shall quote from the report of the Bureau of Municipal Research, in their investigation of the Indian Bureau, published by them in the September issue, 1915, No. 65, "Municipal Research," 261 Broadway, New York City.

This report is just as good for our use today as when it was first made, for very little, if any, change has been made in the administration of Indian Affairs since then.

Prefatory Note

"While this report was printed for the information of members of Congress, it was not made a part of the report of the Joint Commission of Congress, at whose request it was prepared, and is not available for distribution."

Unpublished Digest of Statutory and Treaty Provisions of Governing Indian Funds

"When in 1913 inquiry was made into the accounting and reporting methods of the Indian Office by the President's Commission on Economy and Efficiency, it was found there was no digest of the provisions of statutes and treaties with Indian tribes governing Indian funds and the trust obligations of the government. Such a digest was therefore prepared. It was not completed, however, until after Congress adjourned March 4, 1913. Then, instead of being published, it found its way into the pigeon-holes in the Interior Department and the Civil Service Commission, where the working papers and unpublished reports of the commission were ordered stored. The digest itself would make a document of about three hundred pages."

Unpublished Outline of Organization

"By order of the President, the commission, in cooperation with various persons assigned to this work, also prepared at great pains a complete analysis of the organization of every department, office and commission of the federal government as of July 1, 1912. This represented a complete picture of the government as a whole in summary outline; it also represented an accurate picture of every administrative bureau, office, and of every operative or field station, and showed in his working relation each of the 500,000 officers and employes in the public service. The report in typewritten form was one of the working documents used in the preparation of the 'budget' submitted by President Taft to Congress in February, 1913. The 'budget' was ordered printed by Congress, but the cost thereof was to be charged against the President's appropriation. There was not enough money remaining in this appropriation to warrant the printing of the report on organization. It, therefore, also found repose in a dark closet."

Too Voluminous to Be Made Part of this Series

"Congress alone could make the necessary provision for the publication of these materials; the documents are too voluminous to be printed as a part of this series, even if official permission were granted. It is again suggested, however, that the data might be made readily accessible and available to students by placing in manuscript division of the Library of Congress one copy of the unpublished reports and working papers of the President's Commission on Economy and Efficiency. This action was recommended by the commission, but the only official action taken was to order that the materials be placed under lock and key in the Civil Service Commission."

Need for Special Care in Management

"The need for special care in the management of Indian Affairs lies in the fact that in theory of law the Indian has not the rights of a citizen. He has not even the rights of a foreign resident. The Indian individually does not have access to the courts; he can not individually appeal to the administrative and judicial branches of the public service for the enforcement of his rights. He himself is considered as a ward of the United States. His property and funds are held in trust. * * * The Indian Office is the agency of the government for administering both the guardianship of the Indian and the trusteeship of his properties."

Conditions Adverse to Good Administration

"The legal status of the Indian and his property is the condition which makes it incumbent on the government to assume the obligation of protector. What is of special interest in this inquiry is to note the conditions under which the Indian Office has been required to conduct its business. In no other relation are the agents of the government under conditions more adverse to efficient administration. The influence which make for the infidelity to trusteeship, for subversion of properties and funds, for the violation of physical and moral welfare have been powerful. The opportunities and inducements are much greater than those which have operated with ruinous effect on other branches of public service and on the trustees and officers of our great private corporations. In many instances, the integrity of these have been broken down."

Government Machinery Inadequate

" * * * Behind the sham protection, which operated largely as a blind to publicity, have been at all times great wealth in the form of Indian funds to be subverted; valuable lands, mines, oil fields, and other natural resources to be despoiled or appropriated to the use of the trader; and large profits to be made by those dealing with trustees who were animated by motives of gain. This has been the situation in which the Indian Service has been for more than a century—the Indian during all this time having his rights and properties to greater or less extent neglected; the guardian, the government, in many instances, passive to conditions which have contributed to his undoing."

Opportunities Still Present

"And still, due to the increasing value of his remaining estate, there is left an inducement to fraud, corruption, and institutional incompetence almost beyond the possibility of comprehension. The properties and funds of the Indians today are estimated at not less than one thousand millions of dollars. There is still a great obligation to be discharged, which must run through many years. The government itself owes many millions of dollars for Indian moneys which it has converted to its own use, and it is of interest to note that it does not know and the officers do not know what is the present condition of the Indian funds in their keeping."

Primary Defects

"* * * The story of the mismanagement of Indian Affairs is only a chapter in the history of the mismanagement of corporate trusts. The Indian has been the victim of the same kind of neglect, the same abortive processes, the same malpractices as have the life insurance policyholders, the bank depositor, the industrial and transportation shareholder. The form of organization of the trusteeship has been one which does not provide for independent audit and supervision. The institutional methods and practices have been such that they do not provide either a fact basis for official judgment or publicity of facts which, if made available, would supply evidence of infidelity. In the operation of this machinery, there has not been the means provided for effective official scrutiny and the public conscience could not be reached."

Ample Precedents to Be Followed

"Precedents to be followed are ample. In private corporate trusts that have been mismanaged a basis of appeal has been found only when some favorable circumstance has brought to light conditions so shocking as to cause those people who have possessed political power, as a matter of self-protection, to demand a thorough reorganization and revision of methods. The same motive has lain back of legislation for the Indian. But the motive to political action has been less effective, for the reason that in the past the Indians who have acted in self-protection have either been killed or placed in confinement. All the machinery of government has been set to work to repress rather than to provide adequate means for justly dealing with a large population which had no political rights."

THE LANGUAGE OF STRING

BY KIM SHUCK

THE LANGUAGE OF STRING

It's possible that I could be considered a native speaker of the language of string. It was years before I knew that not everyone beaded, sewed, embroidered, did string figures, braided, knotted, and wove things. Somewhere my mother still has a dishrag improbably scribbled on with violent, overlong, dark maroon stitches of embroidery cotton. When I created that piece, I'm pretty sure that I wasn't in a conventional school yet. My maternal grandma was just about patient enough to walk me through that making. I stabbed my fingers with the embroidery needle so often that over half a century later I can close my eyes and feel the punctures in my fingertips. It was the beginning of understanding.

Woke thinking about where a culture is flexible
Where the human frictions make it stiff make
New poems for the day
Say them to whatever water is listening
Eat and
Throw the doors open to let the
Busy and sketching breeze
Browse the beads

Beads are picked up one by one, and the way that I do it, they are stitched down in threes or fives. When I'm beading, I know that I'm doing a thing that other Cherokees have done, that members of the Polish side of my family have done, that people have done in all kinds of places for years. It may be true that beading has become a shorthand for Indigenous identity, but it's not the glass that defines us. We take up the stories of our cultures. We take up the stories of our time, of all times. We take those stories, act on them with our current understandings, and passions, and perspectives to explain self, to find self. We do this as people always do, taking weaving patterns and translating them to beads, taking nylon thread to replace sinew or, later, cotton, taking new imagery to mean things that are of core importance in a line that goes back before language. I bead to find myself there. I bead cars onto my dance shoes. I bead maps on my friend's shoes. I bead import birds on power lines for a distant cousin. We wear these shoes into dance.

Gesture that settles the shawl on the
Shoulders that
Ensures it will sway in just that way for an
Intertribal an
Auntie gesture a
Preparation to set the world into balance one
Fringe-flick at a
Time

Before anyone decides that dancing isn't important, the US Government banned our dances under the 1883 Religious Crimes Code. I think that they were most alarmed by the Ghost Dance and the Sun Dance. Don't for a moment believe that this code was just a gesture. In part, the Wounded Knee Massacre of 1890 happened because those nearly 300 Lakota people had been dancing. In more recent times, Chilean women have danced the cueca as an act of protest at the disappearance of their loved ones. During the protests about George Floyd's murder there were dance protests including Dance for George an event that took place in Harlem. Dance is a powerful embodied ritual, and the sacred things that we bring there are important: dance shoes, photos of absent and cherished people, the shapeshifting and sometimes wounded pieces of our cultures.

Tectonic plates as
Safe a space to stand as we can
Find and we
Spin and step to the
Rattles on our ankles
Each stone in the

Turtle shell a
Memory or
Lesson

When Zitkala-Ša writes about her mother beading, school experiences, coming back home and finding things had changed, that was her life. It's a gift to have her words about those things. There are still Indigenous lives in progress. For the Dakota, they have her writing to figure out what the generations between have retained through what has been an incredibly difficult time. Cultures change naturally, but no one can claim that the changes in Dakota lives in the last century have been natural. The tectonic plates of culture have shifted faster and more unpredictably than usual and the writers and artists have had to create new protocols and traditions to cover the gap.

The same is true of my people. Cherokee lives have changed through the actions of other cultures. Writing my life today, some of the same stories, some of the old traditions, some of the cultural values remain, but I might see them in different ways. This week I am writing about taking care of aging relatives, coping with writing contracts, and managing a calendar that looks a bit like one of those red string maps in a movie about a serial killer. This is also the dance. We bring what sacred responsibilities and cultural equipment we have to the moment and we move with whatever grace and curiosity we can muster. We have good examples and great scaffolding and most of all our young people today are not less than our ancestors. We will rewrite, re-dance and retake the threads of our lives so that we can pass them on as we always have.

OUR MISSION Founded in 1982, Aunt Lute Books is an intersectional, feminist press dedicated to publishing literature by those who have been traditionally underrepresented in or excluded by the literary canon. Core to Aunt Lute's mission is the belief that the written word is critical to understanding and relating to each other as human beings. Through the centering of voices, perspectives, and stories that have not been traditionally welcomed by mainstream publishing, we strengthen ties across cultures and experiences, promoting a broader range of expression, and, we hope, working toward a more inclusive and just future.

LAND ACKNOWLEDGMENT We, Aunt Lute Books, acknowledge that we do our work of uplifting marginalized voices and striving toward justice via the written word on the unceded ancestral homeland of the Ramaytush Ohlone who are the original inhabitants of the San Francisco Peninsula. As the indigenous stewards of this land and in accordance with their traditions, the Ramaytush Ohlone have never ceded, lost, nor forgotten their responsibilities as the caretakers of this place, as well as for all peoples who reside in their traditional territory. As Guests, we recognize that we benefit from living and working on their traditional homeland. We wish to pay our respects by acknowledging the Ancestors, Elders and Relatives of the Ramaytush Community and by affirming their sovereign rights as First Peoples.

You may buy books from our website.

www.auntlute.com

aunt lute books
P.O. Box 410687
San Francisco, CA 94141
books@auntlute.com

This book would not have been possible without the kind contributions of the Aunt Lute Founding Friends:

Anonymous Donor
Anonymous Donor
Rusty Barceló
Marian Bremer
Marta Drury
Diane Goldstein
Diana Harris
Phoebe Robins Hunter
Diane Mosbacher, M.D., Ph.D.
Sara Paretsky
William Preston, Jr.
Elise Rymer Turner

www.ingramcontent.com/pod-product-compliance
Lightning Source LLC
Jackson TN
JSHW080218020926
107091JS00001B/1